Barrier Islands

Jeffrey Anderson

Published by Jeffrey Anderson, 2024.

Barrier Islands
by
Jeffrey Anderson

First published as an ebook on Smashwords.com
Copyright 2016 by Jeffrey Anderson

This story is a work of fiction.
Names, characters, places, and incidents either are the product of the
author's imagination or are used fictitiously.

This is a work of fiction. Similarities to real people, places, or events are entirely coincidental.

BARRIER ISLANDS

First edition. November 1, 2024.

Copyright © 2024 Jeffrey Anderson.

ISBN: 979-8224928668

Written by Jeffrey Anderson.

To Becky and Summer

1

Brooke Fulcher Howard sat on the blanket spread on the sand gazing at the black ocean in the night. At first it seemed there wasn't much to feel and absorb. The sound of the surf breaking at the first bar twenty yards offshore, the warm marsh-laden breeze out of the west, the fluffy gray-tinged clouds racing past on the horizon east, even the rocking-horse moon settling in the south were all of a dream, a vast all-encompassing soothing dream of rest. Had Brooke been of an introspective sort, she would have found this an odd dream for a twenty-two year old woman.

Then a slash of silver like a meteor's streak only down at the horizon cut across the murmuring ocean and was gone. The sight evoked a gasp, stirring her from the daze. She laughed at herself, more for the idle dream than for the sudden fright that woke her from it. Without looking she reached out to her right and found the anchor of Jodie's foot cased in the pink bootie Miss Polly, Jodie's paternal great-grandmother, had knit for her.

"Your Daddy is showing off," Brooke said as if her daughter could understand though Jodie was only six and a half months old and asleep in any case. "What do you think of a guy surfing in the dark in November with a shark sighting just last week?" She shook her head and chuckled. "But that's what he wanted to do on our anniversary—*our* anniversary! He's out there surfing, and I am left to sit here in the dark watching over you." The baby was lying in her collapsible canvas and metal-tube cradle that Bridge Howard, her paternal grandfather, had fashioned from his garage full of junk with the hand-painted sign *Wind and Wave Salvage* out front.

It was Brooke and Onion's first anniversary. Onion's real name was Roger Howard, but he'd been known as Onion to everyone on Shawnituck Island since his days breading onion rings as a youngster in

JEFFREY ANDERSON

the family restaurant. It was November 20th, certainly late in the season to be doing anything in the water. But the day, which had been bright and surprisingly hot, had given way to a warm evening. And when Brooke had asked what he wanted to do for their anniversary, Onion had tied a pirate's skull and crossbones kerchief over her eyes and led her by one hand while she carried Jodie on her shoulder and he carried who knows what all else in his other arm along the twisting paths from the converted garage where they were living behind his parents' house through the sand roads and across the paved highway—the only pavement on the island— and over the dunes to the beach sloping to the ocean.

Of course Brooke knew where they were going, knew every step of this path from her many times traversing it at all hours of the day and in every weather, sometimes alone, sometimes with Onion, more recently with Jodie on her hip or shoulder, finding her way to the closest approach of the sea, to her place of peace and regeneration amidst all the trials of her life. But this night, with Onion's hand leading her blind, she thought of the first time she'd been led down this path, led by this same hand and blindfolded then too, that time carrying nothing but each other and the seed of love that would be planted as they sat on that same beach in that same dark, June that time, only their hands touching, nothing more, as they talked quietly and then sometimes not at all and stared off toward the vast and gently murmuring ocean.

This time she was carrying her daughter, and whatever Onion was carrying made him winded by the time they cleared the top of the final dune and stumbled downward to a spot partway to the ocean. He let go of her hand and ran off without even stopping to untie her blindfold let alone help her spread out the blanket and assemble the cradle that he'd dropped when he took off. She had to do that alone while keeping Jodie from getting sand in her diaper.

BARRIER ISLANDS

Yet she someway dodged annoyance at Onion's insensitivity, insulated or entranced by that memory of the first night down that path to this spot. She let the warm and soothing salt breeze carry her mind back to her original vision of this island as home to her future, a future that blended seamlessly with the touch of the boy that would become her husband and father of her child. Her dream progressed seamlessly to her half-memory half-idealized vision of this boy rising above her in the dark for them both to claim their prize.

A scream shattered her dream and cleaved the darkness. Something thrashed in the water just off shore then another scream. A dark shape silhouetted by the moonlight stumbled out of the surf and collapsed.

Brooke leapt to her feet. "Onion?" she yelled. "What's wrong?"

"Help me," a weak voice croaked. "Brookie, help me!"

"Onion!" Brooke screamed. She ran toward the figure writhing by the waterline. Though she was running as fast as she could, her feet seemed to get stuck in the sand at each step, making the short jog interminable. The night was throwing off sparks in every direction. "Onion!"

Finally she reached her husband. She knelt beside his body and gently rolled him onto his back. He said nothing. Was he in shock? Was he dead? He had on a wetsuit over his swimming trunks. It was cool and slick and shiny in the dark. She grabbed his bare ankles and gently pulled his two legs out straight. They moved normally, no breaks or obvious injury there. She slid her hands up over his thighs and waist and stomach, fearing that at any moment she'd come upon a gaping wound or a protruding bone. But nothing—all felt normal. Then she reached his arms. The left was fine—floppy but intact. She crossed his chest to the right. But there was no right arm. The wetsuit's shoulder and sleeve were empty, just loose rubber. She gasped. She thought she'd throw up. Her mind raced. Where was the nearest help? How long would it take to summon? How could she leave him, but how could she get help without leaving him?

JEFFREY ANDERSON

"Brookie," he moaned. "Brookie, save me." The words trailed off to silence.

Brooke leaned over, pressed her mouth close to his ear. "Tell me what to do!" she hissed.

"Save me."

She pressed her lips to his cheek. It was surprisingly warm, warmer than her lips, warmer than anything in the night.

At her kiss he groaned and rolled onto his stomach. He thrashed around in the sand. She wanted to hold him but feared she might get hurt or she might hurt him. She started to cry. She was watching her husband in his death throes.

Then the thrashing stopped and the body lay utterly still. She was afraid to touch it. After an excruciatingly long pause, the body rolled over and sat up. Onion, both arms now properly fitted in the wetsuit's sleeves, reached forward and hugged his wife. "You saved my life, Brookie!" he cried. "How can I ever repay you?" Then he burst out laughing.

Brooke pushed him away and leapt to her feet. "You jerk!"

He fell backward in the sand, his laughter coming out in shrieks.

"You freaking jerk!"

Between gasps for air, he managed to say, "You saved me. Your kiss reattached my arm." Then he collapsed in a new spasms of laughter.

Behind her, Brooke could hear Jodie crying. She kicked sand toward her prostrate husband then turned to the sound of her baby's cries. Jodie was hungry and needed to be fed. The timer in Brooke's body already knew this fact, as somewhere in all the commotion her breasts had begun to leak into her padded maternity bra.

She'd just finished nursing Jodie when Onion's wetsuit shiny in the moonlight resolved itself from the inky dark and came up to where she sat. He dropped his surfboard beside the blanket, tossing a light

BARRIER ISLANDS

spray of cool sand across her feet and legs. She grunted in disgust but didn't say anything as she pushed her face into the soft feathers of her daughter's hair, breathing in the soothing aroma of baby shampoo and talcum powder. Jodie was already drifting back to sleep, led there by her now full stomach and the embracing dark.

Onion flopped down on the thin strip of available blanket, his wetsuit brushing against her near shoulder.

"Don't touch me!" she growled in a fierce whisper.

"Aww, come on, Brookie! You got to admit it was pretty funny."

"You scaring me to death isn't funny!"

"You saved me, Baby! Maybe I hadn't got bit by a shark, but you still saved me. It's like a symbol for our love, how you came out here and made me whole. That's my anniversary vow."

Brooke lifted her face from Jodie's hair and looked at him. He faced her from a foot away. His skin was pale and silver in the moonlight, his black hair slicked back and gleaming like a halo. She wondered again how much of this was vision, how much real. "A metaphor."

"Yeah, a metaphor, a symbol for our love."

She faced forward, toward the ocean lapping invisible in the near distance. "Next time send a dozen roses." She made no move to touch him. Jodie was still on her chest. But her tone had softened.

"Where am I going to get roses in November out here?"

She didn't say anything. She clung to Jodie to keep from surrendering.

He leapt up and disappeared into the dark.

She shook her head and cooed to her floppy headed sleeping baby. Then she set Jodie gently in the canvas cradle.

Onion returned carrying a large bouquet of dune grass tassels held together by a woven reed band. He got down on one knee, held out the bouquet, and said, "Brooke Renee Fulcher, would you be my lawful wedded wife, to have and to hold in sickness and in health, for richer and for poorer, from this day forward?"

Brooke hesitated before accepting the bouquet. "I will," she whispered.

Onion then took her left hand, gently prized her loose fist open, and said, "With this ring I plight thee my troth." He slid a shell over the knuckle of her ring finger and pushed it against the simple gold band. "Let this ring be a symbol of our undying love."

Brooke laughed. "A metaphor."

Onion said, "That too."

Brooke rolled the shell ring around on her finger. It was a perfect fit. "How did you find this in the dark?"

"Cat's eyes."

She thought a moment. "Did you have this stuff stowed behind the dune?"

Onion was silent.

"Did you have this planned all along?"

"My lips are sealed," he said, still kneeling in front of her, like her prince emerging real from her dream.

She set her bouquet to one side and reached forward to take his hands in hers. She pulled him toward her till his sealed lips touched hers. She slowly fell backwards to lie on the blanket, making sure his body followed to its rest atop her. She discovered then that he'd somewhere shed his wetsuit and was clothed only in his nylon bathing suit. This made the subsequent series of actions, another metaphor, far simpler than it would have been with the tight-fitting wetsuit.

When they'd completed the consummation of his vows, he rolled off and exhaled to the night and the stars.

She twined the fingers of one hand in his loose counterpart and found Jodie's booty-clad foot with her other hand. She was happy but also very hungry. "Did you bring anything to eat, Mister Sneaky?"

He snorted. "How many hands do you think I have?"

"You had enough a minute ago."

"That helper isn't load-rated for heavy lifting."

BARRIER ISLANDS

"If it can't carry a lunchbox, what good is it?"

"Want me to show you again?"

Her hand drifted to the fork in his legs, the nest of charms he'd covered with his loose swimsuit. "I'm tempted to call your bluff, but first I need something to eat."

"I thought we'd go by the restaurant on our way back and grab some take-out."

"That's good, because I haven't cooked anything."

"So who's the Sneaky now?"

"Wives don't cook dinner on their first anniversary."

"Says who?"

"The Bible."

"Missed that commandment."

"It's there."

Onion sat up and reached into his canvas knapsack. "How about sharing a doobie on their first anniversary?" He passed a crudely rolled joint under her nose.

She'd quit smoking pot soon as she knew she was pregnant and continued the prohibition after Jodie was born for fear of making her baby stoned through her breast milk. "I don't know, Onion."

"Come on, Brookie. You splitting a doobie isn't going to make Jodie retarded." He lit the joint and took a long drag, then offered it to her.

She hesitated then said, "No more retarded than the DNA from her one-armed shark-bit father." She sat up and took the joint.

He released the air smoke from his lungs, coughed once, then said hoarsely, "My thoughts exactly."

"A metaphor," Brooke said, before taking a long hit off the joint.

"Yeah."

JEFFREY ANDERSON

Onion dropped his surfboard, the collapsed cradle, and his slimy wetsuit at the foot of the side steps leading up to the restaurant's front porch. Brooke, with the awake again and wide-eyed Jodie on her hip and the canvas tote over her shoulder, paused at the foot of the steps. "Why don't you go in and get dinner. I'll head back to the house, change Jodie, and put out some plates."

"But I don't know what you want."

"The usual"—by which she meant fried clam strips, onion rings, and slaw.

"You know Miss Polly will be mad if she doesn't get to snuggle Peach Pie." Miss Polly was Onion's grandmother and owner of the restaurant, and Peach Pie was her nickname for Jodie.

Brooke glanced around the restaurant's entry. Though the parking lot was full, there was no line on the porch or inside the foyer; so Miss Polly wouldn't be busy seating customers. She'd probably already spotted them (she has eyes in the back of her head, Brooke well knew from her days of waitressing), and there'd be hell to pay if she snuck off with the baby without saying hi. She looked down over her rumpled shorts and smudged gray sweatshirt, and she knew her hair—formerly in a short boyish crop but now letting it grow out shoulder-length like before she'd come to Shawnituck—must be a tangled mess. "I must look a fright," she said in half-hearted resistance.

"Since when did that matter?" Then he noted her frown and deftly bent and kissed the side of her face, nibbling gently on her ear before he rose back up. "You'll always be the pearl in my oyster," he whispered.

She gave in. "Just for a minute."

He laughed. "Of course."

"Yeah, sure." She dropped the tote beside the surfboard at the bottom of the steps. She considered digging out her worn sandals but decided not to bother. Onion did pull on his tie-dyed t-shirt but remained barefoot also. Had he even brought shoes? They walked up the steps and across the wide porch. The boards were rough and splintery; but with their feet callused from months going barefoot, they didn't notice.

Inside, the bright foyer with Sanford Jones' watercolors hanging on the walls was unusually empty and quiet. This shocked Brooke. She knew from her stint as a waitress that Miss Polly *never* left the cash register unattended. But there it was, unguarded, sitting atop the glass-sided counter with the ship in a bottle displayed below. Brooke turned and looked into the dining room—really, two rooms with a wide wood-framed arched opening in the middle. The tables were all set and laid out but there were no diners seated at them.

"What the heck?" she said. Without waiting for Onion, she strode across the entry foyer to the open doorway leading into the dining room.

"Surprise!" What seemed a hundred voices shouted in unison, followed by the racket of whistling party horns and kazoos and accompanied by thrown confetti and streamers. A sign reading *Happy Anniversary Brooke and Onion* hung across the back wall over the windows that looked out onto the now dark harbor.

Before she could turn and curse her husband for leading her into this trap, she and the baby were swallowed by the crowd of well-wishers, with Miss Polly leading the way followed closely by Onion's parents, Bridge and Lil, and his younger sister.

"Let me see my slice of Peach Pie," Miss Polly said as she lifted Jodie off Brooke's hip and held her up to the crowd like a trophy. "Now I got my great-grandbaby, you can finally eat!" she shouted.

All the crowd cheered.

"Almost had a mutiny," Miss Polly said to Onion over Brooke's shoulder. "Where have you been?"

Onion laughed. "You know how Brookie is about her hair and make-up."

Brooke kicked him in the shin without turning around.

"Oww," he cried but also managed to find a little opening between her sweatshirt and shorts and slide a finger under the waistband. His hand remained there as he came alongside her and together they waded into the crowd of well-wishers.

Awhile later after they got separated (and who knows where Jodie was), Brooke was cornered by Malcolm White who was again trying to convince her to help him start a line of "island" shell jewelry (it would be bought from some overseas supplier) in his small gift shop. "You choose and manage the inventory; I'll provide the shelf space; we split the proceeds," he said with his usual blend of enthusiasm and authority.

Brooke wondered if he and Polly had had a fling. Malcolm was decades younger than Polly, but they sure shared that overbearing and imperious manner. Maybe he was her son, she thought for the first time. Then she laughed to herself. That would be impossible. Out here it was O.K. for a man to sow his seeds wherever he could find a willing partner, but heaven forbid if a women became pregnant with the fruit of those seeds. Then it was the altar or off the island—voluntarily or not on either choice. There were no other options. "I told you, Malc—we don't have the money to invest." She was the only youngster who called him by his first name. All the island kids called him Mr. White with an air of fear or respect depending on the situation.

"Polly would give you a loan."

"I'm not taking money from my in-laws."

"Greta then."

Greta was Brooke's mother's younger sister, an unmarried island immigrant of twenty years standing who made a scratch living painting watercolors and framing them with shells and driftwood for sale in island gift shops. She was Brooke's connection to Shawnituck. Brooke had come here the summer before last, between her sophomore and junior years at Center, to live with Greta and find a summer job. She found the job (at this restaurant) and then Onion and never left. "I'm not going to ask Greta for money either." Where was Greta, anyway? Brooke hadn't seen her for days. Was she feuding with Polly again or shacked up with Andy at his light-keeper's house?

"Your parents?"

Brooke laughed at that. Her mainland parents, safely couched in their country-club lifestyle, had quietly distanced themselves following the wedding. Momma still sent newsy letters once a month, and Brooke responded with sterilized accounts of island life and a few snapshots of the fast-growing Jodie. But neither Momma nor Father had been out there since the wedding and had only seen Jodie at the mainland hospital after she was born. Brooke planned to correct that situation by going home at Christmas, with or without Onion. "Malc, give up. I'm not a salesgirl or a businesswoman."

"Got to do something, and out here it's sea or sales," he said, repeating his favorite slogan.

Just then Onion's younger sister Daphne, nicknamed Daffy, used a plate brimming with items off the buffet to wedge her way between Mr. White and Brooke. "You must be starving," she said to Brooke. "I brought you a plate."

Brooke had all but forgot the original reason they'd stopped at the restaurant (or what she thought had been the reason). But on seeing—and, more importantly, smelling—the plate of fried clams and pork barbecue and French fries and slaw and hushpuppies, she realized she was ravenous. "For me?" she exclaimed, genuinely touched at Daffy's thoughtfulness. Since marrying Onion and settling into their garage apartment, she'd lost the newcomer status and favors she'd enjoyed that first summer. Now it was, most times, serve yourself or don't get served at all.

"Let the girl eat," Daffy told Mr. White with an uncommon assertiveness. She was the only student in the senior class of the K through 12 island school across from the church in the center of the village. She was homely but bright, bashful but inquisitive; and she looked to Brooke for hints of the world beyond the island.

Brooke turned toward Daffy, leaned over and delicately kissed her sister-in-law on each cheek, then took the plate of food. By the time she turned back, Malc White had moved on to some other prey—in this case Lorelei Bradford, immigrant wife of island native Sloop Bradford. She owned the shop across from Malc's, and he was pressing her to merge. Brooke breathed a sigh of relief for both the escape and the food. "You're a darling," she said.

Daffy smiled broadly, her large mouth suddenly dominating her face in a manner that was simultaneously endearing and haunting. "I wouldn't be much good at a water rescue, but I can lifeguard with the best at a party."

"Didn't know you had such talent," Brooke said between French fries.

Daffy lost her smile and glanced to the floor. "Lots of things you don't know about me."

Brooke looked at her sister-in-law's dull taupe-colored hair. Some blond highlights would do wonders, and a volumnizing conditioner and maybe some rouge on her cheeks. These were products from a bygone mainland existence, when appearances dominated daily life and preparations. She no longer used (or could afford) them herself, but suddenly wanted them for Daffy. "Like your college plans?"

Daffy looked up with a fresh glint in her eyes. "You went to Center, right?"

Center was the main campus of the state-operated college system. As its name implied, it was near the center of the state, a world away from remote Shawnituck in distance and lifestyle. "Two years."

"Major?"

Brooke laughed. "Partying."

Daffy frowned.

BARRIER ISLANDS

"Biology," Brooke corrected. "Though I was thinking of switching into the new computer science department before I washed ashore out here."

"Really? I want to be a vet. That's pre-med, right?"

"I think so."

"Must be tough."

"You could do it." Brooke suddenly wanted success, and a life beyond the island, for her reticent sister-in-law.

"You think so?"

"I'm sure of it."

"Do you know anyone at Center who could help me get in?"

Brooke laughed. "Probably don't want to use me as a reference."

"Why?"

"Let's just say there were a few incidents that didn't exactly endear Brooke Fulcher to the school's administration."

"Nothing too awful?"

"Just student pranks."

"I'd love to go to Center."

"Then do it."

"Daddy would never agree."

"Why not?" Bridge had always been kind to Brooke and seemed more open-minded than most of the island's natives.

"He says I'm too naïve."

"What's he want you to do?"

"Stay here."

"And?"

"And marry some island boy, have more grandchildren."

Brooke glanced around the room and spotted Jodie, cradled in her mother-in-law Lil's arms. As if on cue, Bridge bent over his only grandchild to-date and tickled her stomach. Jodie's face scrunched up in what was surely a giggle, inaudible amidst all the talk and laughter; her tiny hands reached out and pulled her Pap's whiskers. He laughed in delight, that low bellow rumbling across the room. At just that moment, Brooke felt a trickle of wetness high on her inner thigh, the real leavings of her dream-like tryst with Onion on the beach. She shivered with something akin to terror at the thought that Bridge's second grandchild might already be started.

2

The next morning Brooke bundled up Jodie and headed out for Greta's cottage a quarter mile away through narrow sand lanes. A dense and cold fog had settled over the island, a not uncommon occurrence this time of year as cold air mixed with the warm water. It made the island, already set off from the mainland and the twentieth century, seem all that much more isolated. It would have been easy for Brooke, raised on scary stories and screamer movies, to imagine all sorts of frightening things hiding in the fog. But she was a parent now, and parents didn't indulge in frivolous anxieties. It was a different fear, one still buried deep in her unconscious, that unsettled her as she wrapped Jodie in the soft Shetland wool blanket and then used Bridge's spare oil-cloth shrimper's hat as a tent to keep the mist off her baby. She was not near so conscientious about protecting herself, simply pulling on a hooded gray sweatshirt over her t-shirt and khaki shorts, leaving her legs and feet bare. One of the great liberations of living out here was being free to go barefoot year-round—well, at least nine months out of the year. And it wasn't yet December.

Greta's cottage set off by itself on the sound-side. It's only land-side approach was by a narrow path between dense head-high boxwood hedges. She bought it as a fisherman's shack a year after moving out here using a small inheritance from her grandmother, then traded labor and other favors with local craftsmen to upgrade it to year-round usage. It was now quaint and charming and cozy but also very "Greta," filled with small paintings taped to the wall and knickknacks that had the feel of folk craft and art but were most likely just items she'd collected from trash bins and flea markets on her occasional trips to the mainland.

Brooke and her living bundle stepped into the screened entry porch. She hung Bridge's rain cap, now dripping wet, on a peg, checked to confirm that Jodie was dry, felt that she was and also saw that she was asleep. She set the baby gently on the slat-wood swing, then shook herself off and wiped herself down using the somewhat dry sleeve of the sweatshirt. This process rattled the floor of the cottage, as she knew it would, and brought her aunt to the front door.

Greta opened the door with a scowl. "What in the world, child?"

"Hi, Greta!"

"Don't you know there are spirits live in this fog?"

"I hope so."

"Best not, child. Nuff to battle out here without putting them in the mix. Least you didn't bring little Jo-jo out."

"But I did, Greta. Look!" She gestured to the bundle wrapped like a mummy resting on the swing.

"My Lord!" Greta exclaimed, though her broad grin betrayed her words.

She leaned over with Brooke to peer at the infant. Brooke gently eased back the fringe of the blanket to uncover Jodie's pale face. With her closed eyes, downturned mouth, and slightly furrowed brow, she looked like a shrunken old man.

"See," Greta whispered. "Spirits took her."

"Naw. She's just asleep." Brooke ran her finger ever so lightly over her baby's cheek. Jodie responded by moving her lips as if to nurse and mewing faintly, but didn't open her eyes. Something about that combination of gestures in this isolated spot on this shrouded day produced in Brooke a visceral will to protect her one offspring. She was generally attentive to Jodie. But the island's close-knit community, and her in-laws' extensive and insistent clan, tempered individual possessiveness and its flipside, jealousy, in favor of shared ownership and responsibility. That communal character had been much of what had attracted Brooke to Shawnituck. So why this sudden new urge to safeguard her safely sleeping baby?

Greta looked first to the baby then to Brooke. "Let's get inside, child, before you both catch pneumonia."

BARRIER ISLANDS 17

Once inside the cottage's one main room well-warmed by a woodstove of in the corner, Brooke unwrapped Jodie's head and upper body but left the blanket loosely pulled around her legs and cloth-diaper (which still smelled clean). Jodie roused and blinked at the light of the lantern on the kitchen table, then focused her eyes on Greta. Brooke handed the bundle over to her aunt.

"Come here, darling," Greta cooed. She sat gently on the chair pulled out beside the table.

Brooke laughed. Jodie was the only one she'd ever seen who could make Greta instantly lose her cantankerous nature. She'd been told by Momma that Greta had treated her the same way when she was a baby, fawning over and doting on her like she was "the princess of England!" Maybe that was the origin of the special bond she'd always had for her aunt. "Can I make some tea?" Brooke asked.

"Since when do you have to ask?" Greta said.

"Since when I ask if you'd like some."

Greta scoffed. "Never drink the stuff less it's iced and loaded with sugar."

"I know. Just checking." She found the tea bags on the shelf where she'd left them while living here before marrying Onion—a year and a day past. "Missed you at the party last night," she said as she put water in the teapot.

"Didn't know there was a party," Greta said, though she knew very well what her niece was referring to.

Brooke laughed. "Me either. I looked like a beach bum!"

"I'm sure they loved you."

"Who?"

"Them Howards."

"Thought you didn't know there was a party." Brooke caught the kettle just before it whistled and filled the Wedgewood cup with the teabag.

"No party out here without Howards present in force."

Brooke laughed. Greta had ample bluster but she mainly spoke simple truths amidst those gales. Out here, her in-laws were one of two dominant families, along with the Garrisons who controlled the east-end (ocean side) of the village and mostly kept to themselves. Little happened on the sound side without the Howards at least knowing about it, if not initiating it. "They threw a surprise anniversary party for me and Onion at the restaurant. Well, it was a surprise to me. Onion knew about it and led me in there unawares."

"Like a lamb to slaughter," Greta said, though in her quiet cooing voice.

Brooke brought her tea and sat opposite Greta and Jodie. "It wasn't that bad, Greta. The food was good. Everybody was nice."

"Long as you march to the beat of their drum."

Greta had introduced Brooke to Miss Polly and the Howard "hoard" as she called them on Brooke's second day out here. Back then they got along well enough. But a little while after the birth of Jodie, Miss Polly had sent word via an untraceable sequence of intermediaries that she thought it was time for Greta to quit her open-secret liaison with Andy Lawson, the light-keeper, who was still married to a Howard cousin, Judy Lawson, though they hadn't lived together for decades and Judy now kept house with Buck Blackburn. That's when Greta stopped having social contact with the Howards, though she nodded to them when passing in the lanes and still did barter trade in their shops. One couldn't live on Shawnituck and not interact with the Howards to some degree. "Guess I'll be marching to that drum here on out."

"Jodie too?" Greta looked down at the baby cradled in her arms. She was calm and quiet, as if asleep; but her eyes were open, fixed on the wizened, gray-haired face above.

Brooke laughed. "She's Island property now."

Greta's head jerked up as if slapped. "She is not!"

Brooke was used to her aunt's heartfelt declarations; still, this one caught her by surprise with its sudden vehemence. "Her last name is

BARRIER ISLANDS

Howard. She was practically born with sand between her toes. Can't get much more 'island' than that."

"Look at me, Brooke." She waited for her niece to raise her eyes from the now empty cup in her hands. "You are in charge of Jodie's future. You choose—not Polly or Bridge or Onion. You!"

"Jeez, Greta. If I didn't know better, I'd swear you were channeling Momma."

"I was all but raised by your mother, and generally kicking and screaming, or sneaking out the window. But even then I knew Mary was blessed with calm good sense. I just never listened."

"So coming out here was a mistake?"

Greta's eyes lost their spark and flash, and squinted in recall. Her weathered cheeks lifted into a grin. "If you'd seen Andy back then, you'd never use the word 'mistake' to describe my choice to follow him from Coastal back out here. I would have followed him to the ends of the earth."

Brooke laughed. "Back then, Shawnituck was the end of the earth!" Greta had met Andy Lawson at the state-college branch on the coastal plain, when he was a senior and she a sophomore. He'd returned to his home on Shawnituck to marry Judy Howard. Greta had followed in hopes he'd change his mind about the marriage, then chose to stay on anyway.

"So it was," Greta agreed. "Weekly Sound transit on the mail boat if you were willing to sit next to the pigs and chickens."

"Why did you stay?"

Greta considered the question. No one had ever asked her outright, though she'd asked herself many times, the answer changing frequently over the years. "I told myself it was for love."

Brooke laughed. "I know about that one."

Greta fixed her with a fresh hard stare. "Then you know it's a lie."

Brooke didn't answer.

So Greta continued. "Even after he married, I somehow convinced myself he'd leave her and join me. Many a night in this very room before it had windows or wall boards, I'd lay awake on my cot waiting for Andy to appear above me and take me in his arms."

"How romantic," Brooke purred without a trace of irony.

"How foolish!" Greta barked.

"Andy eventually came."

"No, I went to him—after the accident, and Judy had driven him out with her sharp tongue and wandering eye." Andy had shattered his ankle on his father-in-law's shrimp boat. A year or so later, he'd quietly left his wife and childless home and taken up residence at the light-keeper's house next to the island's lighthouse that he tended for a very small government stipend.

"But you love him."

Greta nodded. "I do. That part never changed."

"Then what did?"

"I became this hardened old coot, worn and shaped by this place every bit as much as that live oak out front."

"Why?"

She shrugged. "That's what this island does to you."

"No. Why did you stay?"

"You mean after the glow of romance wore off?"

Brooke nodded.

"Shame, I think. Maybe fear—of failure, of not fitting into the rest of the world. It was easier to be an outcast on a cast-off island than one more spoke in the world's big wheel."

"You make it sound so attractive."

"Mainland?"

"Yes."

"I've always rejected it. No reason to change now—too late anyway."

Brooke nodded, not sure if she felt sorry for or proud of her aunt.

BARRIER ISLANDS

"But not for you," Greta said, then looked down on Jodie, now starting to stir in her blanket wrap. "And certainly not for her."

3

Brooke sat staring at the artificial Christmas tree Onion had set up in the corner of their garage apartment. It had silver branches and a white base and didn't even try to look like a real tree. A year ago when she'd asked about the possibility of a real, live tree, everyone had laughed at the thought, claiming such an extravagance would "cost a King's ransom" to get shipped out here and would likely be salt stained and dried out and dropping its needles even before it got set in the stand. The only family on the island that had a real tree were the O'Rourkes, a wealthy immigrant couple that had built a three-story "mansion" on the furthest point reaching out into the Atlantic and set a tall green tree with abundant lights and ornaments behind their living room's picture window for the whole village to see. When Brooke had commented on how pretty it looked, Onion had sneered that it was probably fake like everything else the O'Rourkes did—all show and no substance. And it was true that nobody from the village ever set foot inside the mansion to verify the authenticity of the tree or anything else within the house. Still, Brooke couldn't help but envy the O'Rourkes their gleaming green tree and imagined the pine scent it surely emitted.

Last year, still in the afterglow of her wedding and caught up in furnishing their cozy apartment and planning for the nursery and their baby's arrival, Brooke had managed to ignore her pangs of holiday homesickness at the absence of her family and its Christmas traditions dating back far as she could remember, including the live tree picked out and cut down by Father with his bow-saw with the red-painted handle at the farm out in the county and ceremoniously hauled in the borrowed pickup back to their house in the city and set in the stand on Christmas Eve afternoon to be decorated just before bedtime on Christmas Eve night with Brooke charged with setting the star on the top of the tree, in the old days while perched atop Father's shoulders but more recently off a step ladder after the year she'd caused a pulled

BARRIER ISLANDS

muscle in Father's neck such that he walked around all Christmas with his head tilted to one side like Quasimodo, though even that memory elicited subsequent gales of laughter each future Christmas as Brooke and her sister Leah would walk around with their heads tilted to one side against their scrunched up shoulders.

But this year, with their apartment fully furnished and feeling cramped and Jodie now more than seven months old and no fresh challenges to distract or occupy her unless changing Jodie's diaper for the thousandth time and washing the poop out in the toilet before setting the diaper to soak in the big galvanized washtub out back qualified as a challenge (though that could hardly be called "fresh" in newness or odor), Jodie could not help but stare at the forlorn fake tree with the stark gaze of disappointment and despair.

And the tree became a convenient symbol of greater holiday-related frustrations. She wanted to collect thoughtful and highly personalized gifts for her baby and Onion and her extensive entourage of in-laws, each of whom would present such a gift to her or Jodie. Most of all, she wanted to acquire such personalized gifts in an island theme to take to her family when she visited them over Christmas. But they didn't have the money for her to buy these gifts and she lacked the creativity of Polly (with crocheting) or Bridge (with metalwork) or Lil (with knitting) or Greta (with painting) to design and create such gifts. Though she'd so often ridiculed the post-Thanksgiving shopping extravaganzas to the malls she and Leah and Momma would take throughout her childhood and adolescence and right up to her last year at home, complaining of the "empty consumerism" and "herd mentality," she now missed that opportunity, partly for the wide selection in gift ideas it provided but mostly for the shared endeavor it defined. There were no malls on the island or anywhere along this part of the coast. And trips to the mainland's cities were involved and stressful, all the more so with preparing and packing up Jodie and her supplies. And in any case, they had no money!

She heard a light tapping on the apartment's only entry door that had once been the side door before the roll-up doors had been removed (saved for later reinstallation) and those openings walled up to make their residence. "It's always open," Brooke yelled, making the double-edged point that the recycled knob's key had been lost ages ago and, as Onion said, "Who locks their doors anyway?"—an island reality that Brooke had originally considered charming but now felt was presumptuous.

Daffy opened the door and stuck her head through the crack. "Mind if I stop in for a few minutes?"

Her sister-in-law's shy and doubtful expression on that pale face with those large dark eyes turned Brooke's frown into a welcoming grin. "Come in. I could use the company."

Daffy's face brightened as she came through the door and sat across the table. "I saw Onion had closing tonight."

"Everybody has to take their turn."

"Got your tree up!"

Brooke snickered. "I guess you can call it that."

"You had a real tree growing up?"

"Every year."

Daffy nodded. "I heard Onion tell Dad. He feels bad you can't have a real tree."

Brooke shrugged. "It's not just the tree. Everything's different."

Daffy laughed. "All seems the same to me—and the same and the same and the same! I'd die for something different."

"Jodie," Brooke said, her expression lifting as she glanced toward the crib where her baby was sleeping.

Daffy smiled too. "Her first Christmas."

"Yes."

"Are you really taking her to the mainland?"

Brooke's jaw tightened. "My parents haven't seen her since she was born."

BARRIER ISLANDS

"I know. I understand. But we'll all miss her Christmas Day, and you too."

"But you'll still have your brother," Brooke said with a note of bitterness. Onion refused to consider leaving the island for Christmas—or any other time for more than doctor's visits.

"He's scared."

"Of what?"

"Of not wanting to come back."

"That's crazy, Daffy. A few days on the mainland isn't going to change your mind about your home. Or if it does, then maybe your mind should be changed."

"You don't have to convince me, but that's not how most folks out here see it. They're afraid if they surrender even a tiny bit, their whole little world will collapse."

"Going to change whether they want it to or not."

"Not without a fight."

Brooke thought of her shouting match with Onion last night over Christmas plans, but one little skirmish in a much larger war. "Got your Christmas shopping done?" She meant it as a joke to change the subject.

"Not much in the way of shopping, but I've got gifts for everyone," she said then added, "Except you." She blushed.

"You don't have to get me anything, Daffy. You don't have any more money than I do."

"Who needs money?"

"Then how?"

Daffy grinned shyly. "Can I show you something I've never shown anyone?"

"Sure."

"You have to come up to my room."

"I'll have to bring Jodie."

"Of course."

26   JEFFREY ANDERSON

Brooke rose and picked Jodie up from her crib, keeping the pink and white Angora wool blanket, hand woven by Onion's aunt, wrapped around her. Jodie opened her eyes but didn't utter a peep. Together they followed Daffy out the door and around the car under the carport to the side door to her in-laws modest two-story house. They scooted through the empty kitchen and went up the narrow stairs and down the hall to Daffy's room. Brooke had been upstairs in this house only a few times, and then only to Onion's room—at first for a little pre-marital frolicking on his narrow bed one weekend when his parents and sister were on the mainland for a friend's wedding, then later to help him pack for the move to the apartment. The rough-board wood ceiling was low and the hall narrow.

Daffy paused in front of her bedroom's door at the end of the hall. "Close your eyes," she said.

Brooke hesitated. "No heart-stopping surprises, O.K.? Not while I've got Jodie." The baby still hadn't uttered a sound.

"No sudden surprises."

Brooke closed her eyes. She heard the door creak open on old hinges then felt Daffy's fingers grasp her free hand and lead her forward. Once inside the room, she heard the door close behind.

"O.K. You can open your eyes."

Brooke opened her eyes but had to blink twice before registering what was before them. The room's ceilings sloped in line with the roof above and had a triangular wall with a single window at the far end. The walls and ceilings, like the hall, were covered with wood boards. Covering almost every inch of those walls and ceilings was a dazzling array of beautiful photographs. Most were landscapes, some close-ups, all richly colored. A quick survey indicated that every picture had a living creature—mammal, fish, bird, insect—as the focal point. Even the wide-angle landscapes—a sunset over the water, the harbor in morning light—had a flying pelican or floating otter as a reminder of animate life. Brooke gasped. "Where did you get these?"

BARRIER ISLANDS

Daffy laughed. "I took them, silly."

"And had them printed?" She was doing a quick tally in her head based on the cost of the mail-order developing and printing of snapshots of Jodie. Those 3 x 5's were expensive enough. She couldn't imagine the price for these 8 x 10's and 11 x 14's.

"Printed them myself."

"Where?"

She blushed and looked away. "Ralph Hopson has a darkroom he lets me use."

Ralph Hopson was one of the teachers at the village school, fresh out of college and working out here on a one-year grant to improve education in the state's out-of-the-way rural communities. He was an energetic and idealistic charmer who had all the young girls and half the middle-aged housewives on the island in a tizzy. Brooke thought of him as a perfect match for her equally idealistic sister, Leah, which of course meant he didn't do anything for her. "Where's his darkroom?"

"He's converted the pantry at his cottage."

"And you can use it?"

"Under his supervision at first." She paused. "Now he lets me use it whenever I want."

Brooke strode over and looked at some of the photos taped to the ceiling more closely. "These are incredible, Daffy. They have so much feeling." She walked slowly down the length of the room, checking out each of the photos. They were all quite striking, but the ones that riveted her attention were close-ups of horses. She eventually realized they had to be of the island's herd of wild horses that occasionally wandered into the village but generally kept to the sea-grass dunes north of town. Tourists would often ask about riding them, which always made the natives laugh, as one couldn't get within twenty yards of those feral beasts let alone saddle or ride one. "Do you have a telephoto lens?" Brooke asked, pausing in front of a close-up of a horse's eye, soft and brown and mysterious, set in a roan-colored cheek.

"I asked for one for Christmas, but I'm not counting on it."

"Then how'd you get so close?"

"You want to see?" Her voice was edged with the excitement of finally sharing long-held secrets—first this room, now another.

Brooke, still awed by this revelation, could only nod in silence.

"We'll have to leave Jodie with Mom."

Brooke had all but forgotten the baby cradled in her arm. But this wasn't unusual—Jodie on her arm or shoulder was by now like a new appendage. She looked to her baby. Her wide eyes were focused at something beyond Brooke's face. She turned and saw the picture of a gull standing as a one-legged sentinel on a rough pier post. "Will she mind?" Brooke asked, though she already knew the answer. Lil took Jodie every chance she got, at times annoying Brooke with her constant requests. She could hear the television droning downstairs, where Bridge was no doubt snoring in his recliner and Lil was knitting on the sofa. She'd happily set Jodie beside her to watch the dance of the knitting needles and listen to their click-click. Jodie got so mesmerized by those needles that Lil claimed she'd be a seamstress or a clothing designer when she grew up.

Daffy laughed. "You're kidding, right?"

"Yeah, I guess."

Twenty minutes later they'd left Jodie with Lil, gone out the house's back door, and snaked their way along a maze of narrow trails through tall thickets. The night was dense-dark, with low clouds hiding any moon or stars. Daffy had a flashlight but didn't turn it on, urging Brooke to stay close and sometimes grabbing her hand to guide her through tight spots in the path. The air was thick and cold with a salt-laden dampness. Daffy had tossed her Onion's fleece-lined field coat as they'd headed out the door; and she was glad she had it, buttoned it all the way to her neck. She was also glad to have on her hiking boots, though they still felt heavy as cinderblocks on her feet used to being unshod.

By the time they reached the small clearing in the brush, Brooke's eyes had adjusted sufficiently to the dark for her to discern not only the clearing but also the silhouettes of animals at the far edge of the clearing. The sharp odor of damp fur and the distinct smell of horse manure identified those silhouettes as the wild horses. Brooke tensed, fearing that the horses might spook and run over them in the dark.

Daffy pressed her hand into Brooke's chest and whispered, "Wait here."

Just then, one of the horses snorted a sharp warning. Brooke had no intention of moving, not even an inch. She felt Daffy's hand drift over her coat then away. Then Daffy moved silently ahead until the skin of her pale face merged into the darker brush at the back edge of the clearing.

What seemed to Brooke a very long interval passed with no sign from Daffy and only the sound of the horses milling slowly to break the absolute stillness of the night. Then suddenly a brilliant light shined at the far edge of the clearing. It was the flashlight illuminating Daffy's face and upper body. She stood amongst the herd of horses, a dozen or more visible in the diffuse light. And right next to Daffy was the roan horse from so many of the photos. She offered the horse a piece of carrot from the pocket of her hooded sweatshirt then patted the horse's cheek as it crunched on the carrot.

"I call her Ruby," Daffy said in a confident but gentle voice. Though in normal volume, her voice sounded like a shout after so much silence. "After Dorothy's slippers. I befriended her two summers ago when she was a foal. Her mother kept trying to shy her away from me, but Ruby was brave and curious enough to check out this two-legged visitor. It took weeks of patience, but eventually she got close enough for me to touch her. Now look." She reached up and scratched behind the horse's long pointed ears.

"And the others?" Brooke asked, still not moving from her spot on the far side of the clearing.

"They've sort of accepted me, but they won't let me touch them. And now I think Ruby's pregnant, and I don't know what will happen if she has a foal."

Brooke could laugh at that. "A baby changes everything."

"So I've heard." Daffy patted the forehead of Ruby, then the flashlight went dark.

A minute later, Daffy was again beside her, materializing out of the deeper dark like a pale ghost. Without a word, and still not using the flashlight, she led Brooke back over the paths to the house.

On the side stoop and in the circle of light from the bare bulb on the wall, it seemed again safe to speak. "So those are your Christmas presents?" Brooke said.

"What? The horses?"

Brooke laughed. "No. The photographs."

Daffy nodded. "Yes. But I need help with the frames. So I've got a deal—if you'll help me put together the frames, I'll let you pick any photos in any sizes to give to your family. They aren't world-class art, but they are unique to the island."

Brooke all but leapt for joy. "That's wonderful, Daffy." She hugged her sister-in-law. "I've watched Greta make her frames. I'm sure she can give us some tips and let us use her scrap wood." She kissed Daffy's cheek. "You're a life saver!"

Daffy blushed then grew serious. "It's our secret."

"The horses?"

"And the photos. I don't want people asking too many questions. O.K.?"

Brooke stared at Daffy and saw at just that moment her sister Leah. And she gave their sign language gesture of absolute secrecy—a cross over her heart followed by a fist closed padlock tight.

BARRIER ISLANDS

Daffy smiled. "Good." She turned to mount the two steps into the house.

Brooke caught Daffy's hand from behind and waited for her to turn. She whispered, "Do you know how I can get condoms without the whole town knowing about it?" Brooke had grown terrified of becoming pregnant again so soon after Jodie. She'd resumed her period two months ago and worried that her anniversary tryst on the beach might've already started a second child in her. Since that night she'd explored means of sexual sharing other than intercourse (much to Onion's surprise and glee) and was relieved beyond words when she began menstruating this morning. Now she needed mechanical birth control until she could get her mainland doctor to put her on the pill. Asking her sister-in-law for help in this regard was a huge leap of trust.

Daffy looked down from the first step with a serene gaze far beyond her years. "I'll see what I can do."

Brooke said, "Our secret, right?"

Daffy smiled and crossed her heart then made a fist.

4

Three days before Christmas and the night before Brooke was scheduled to leave with Jodie for a week at her parents' house, Onion arrived home from closing the restaurant drunk. He sat heavily on their thin double mattress and shook his sleeping wife's shoulder.

Brooke woke and checked the clock on the upturned apple crate that served as their nightstand—1:15. She had waited up till eleven, the time Onion normally got home after closing, then turned out the lights and went to bed. She would have to get up before dawn to get Jodie ready for the trip and get to the ferry dock by 6:30 to hold her reservation on the 7 AM crossing. "Where have you been?" Her voice was a little groggy, but her head was instantly clear and awake.

"Never mind where I've been. Why are you leaving?"

Brooke rolled her face into the pillow to muffle her scream then counted to ten in silence before again facing her husband in the room's dim light from the pole lamp outside their window that Lil always kept on. She said it was to help them come and go in the dark, but Onion had told her long ago that his mother believed the island was inhabited by the spirits of those lost at sea and kept the light on to fend them off. Brooke took a deep breath then said, "My family has not seen Jodie since she was born. I'm going to visit them for a few days."

"What happened to the 'Till death do us part?'"

Brooke had assumed Onion was a little toked on pot. He almost always shared a joint or two with the clean-up crew before locking up. But tonight she smelled rum on his breath. That would explain why he was so late, and where he'd been—to Jack's, the only bar on the island open late this time of year. "You're welcome to come with me. I want you to come with me. I could use the help."

"You promised we'd never spend a night apart."

Early in their romance, Brooke had made Onion promise they would never spend a night apart and sealed it with a pinky swear and

BARRIER ISLANDS

a subsequent twining of other body parts. To keep the vow, Onion had slept in the chair in the hospital room (or tried to) the night before and the night after Jodie's birth. They'd ridden the ferry back together, Onion cradling the blanket-enshrouded Jodie the whole way as Brooke stretched out on the lounge's bench to try to ease the pain of her episiotomy. They'd landed to a hero's homecoming—all the Howards and half the rest of the village assembled on the dock with pink streamers and bows—as Onion emerged down the ramp with their prize and Brooke had followed walking gingerly. Daffy had brought out a wheelchair which Brooke at first declined then gladly accepted. Onion gave her Jodie, to hold on her lap, then took the wheelchair's handles from Daffy and pushed his family through the crowd of well-wishers. When they reached the end of the ferry station's paved walk and looked ahead to the path of soft sand, Brooke had made a move to rise from the wheelchair. But Onion pushed her back down and nodded to two of his cousins. They each grabbed a wheel of the chair and carried her and the newborn all the way through town to Bridge and Lil's house.

"I never promised not to see my family," Brooke said quietly but firmly. They'd had this discussion numerous times in the last month.

"Your home is out here."

"But my family is on the mainland. I'm going to see them for one week—one week out of fifty-two weeks, Onion!" Her voice had crept up in volume and frustration through that brief speech. She glanced toward the crib and was relieved to see no movement there. Jodie would be difficult enough tomorrow without losing sleep tonight.

"And leaving me."

Brooke suddenly felt sorry for her husband. "Please come with us." She brushed his cheek with her hand.

"Your family hates me."

"They don't hate you. They hardly know you. This will be your chance to get to know them."

"It's Christmas, Brooke!"

"Duh."

"I spend Christmas here."

"I spent last Christmas here. We can alternate."

"I don't have a ferry reservation."

Brooke laughed at that one. "Your uncle is the ferry captain!"

"He can't break the rules."

"Since when?"

"Since today."

"Come with us, Onion."

"Don't leave."

"I'm going to see my family."

Onion stood suddenly and headed back out into the night.

He still hadn't returned when Brooke rose at 5:30. She wondered how she'd get Jodie plus all her stuff to the ferry station till Daffy tapped on the door at 6:10. Together they lugged her three bags plus Jodie through the empty village to the station.

Daffy walked with her onto the ferry and helped get Jodie and the bags situated on the bench. She leaned over and hugged Brooke seated below. "Merry Christmas. We'll miss you." She rose up smiling.

Brooke nodded and hoped her thanks showed through her eyes. "Merry Christmas."

"Hurry back. I can't wait to give you my present!"

"This is present enough."

"No. This is just helping a friend."

"Your sister-in-law."

"My friend."

Brooke hesitated then asked, "Am I awful for leaving?"

"You're doing what you have to do."

"And that's O.K.?"

"We do what we have to do."

"Onion?"

"Him too."

"Will he be O.K.?"

She grinned. "He slept in his old room last night."

Brooke sighed. "I don't know if I should be relieved or terrified."

Daffy thought for a moment. "Maybe both." She turned and headed out of the passenger lounge, back into the predawn dark, toward the sleeping village.

5

Two days after Christmas, Brooke left Jodie with Momma and Father after dinner and headed out with her sister Leah for an evening of girl talk and club-hopping. Everything about the evening was unprecedented. Of course it was the first time Brooke had left Jodie alone with her parents, and the first time she'd gone clubbing with Leah (the last time they'd been together at home, almost two years ago, Leah was still underage). It was also the first time that Leah, who was deaf and had grown up highly dependent on her older sister, drove Brooke around. Though she'd had her license for some time before Brooke had moved to Shawnituck, Brooke had always insisted on driving. But tonight Leah had the keys to the family's spare car and simply walked to the driver's side and got in, leaving Brooke momentarily frozen on the sidewalk before she finally opened the passenger door of the Volvo and got in.

You my chauffeur now? Brooke signed.

Leah grinned. *My car, my rules.*

Brooke shrugged. *So where are you taking me?*

You will see. Leah cranked the car.

She took her to a new club downtown called Starburst. As soon as they entered the vestibule, Brooke heard the disco music throbbing though the walls. She grabbed her sister and signed *What do you know about disco?* The last word had no precedent in their signing, so she signed *dance* while saying "disco," as Leah could read lips even faster than signing.

Leah smiled broadly then laid a hand on the nearest wall, felt the percussive beat, closed her eyes, and began a slow and graceful shuffle to the music, ending with a twirl that merged her ballet training to the new disco craze. When she opened her eyes, she discovered Brooke's mouth agape. Leah laughed at her sister's look, the sound a bit too loud for the close space but surprisingly natural and at ease.

BARRIER ISLANDS

It took Brooke a second to realize she'd never heard Leah utter more than a tentative giggle, so afraid was she of sounding foolish or weird.

Leah signed *You taught me!*

Taught you what?

To dance! At the Ball!

When Leah was seventeen, she'd insisted on being presented at the annual debutante ball despite her condition; and Brooke had agreed to be her dance partner for the evening's signature waltz, participating and leading in the dance despite hating ballroom dancing and the very idea of the stuffy debutante ball. And Leah had been the hit of that year's Ball. Brooke laughed at the memory that seemed ages past though it was only three years ago. *But disco?* she mouthed.

Leah shrugged, smiled, then paid their cover and entered the dance hall.

It was a large dimly lit room with tables around the perimeter and an open dance floor in the middle. The floor was lit by flashing multi-colored lights and the strobe effect of a mirror ball rotating above. Though not full, Brooke was surprised to see a decent crowd, including a number of familiar faces from high school, on this weeknight during Christmas break. Leah pulled her to a silver table at the far side of the room. A card on the table read "Reserved for Leah and Brooke." Leah waved to the woman behind the bar; she smiled and nodded back. They sat down. A waitress brought them drinks—club soda for Leah, a wine cooler for Brooke—and a bowl of pretzels.

"I'm Marie," the waitress said. "You must be Brooke."

Brooke shook her hand. "Usually. But tonight I guess I'm Leah's sister."

The waitress laughed. "That too." She looked to Leah and spoke to her eyes. "Everyone here loves Leah."

Leah blushed, visible despite the dim light.

"And she can dance!"

Leah laughed and signed *With the right partner.*

"Most anybody here—girls or guys. They love to dance with Leah."

Leah signed *Tonight I am here with my sister.*

"You can teach her to dance."

"No way. I'll watch," Brooke said.

Leah smiled. *Talk tonight.*

The waitress shrugged. "Suit yourself. Tony says 'hi'—bought you this round."

Both Leah and Brooke looked up to the guy behind the bar. It was Tony Douglas, a classmate of Brooke's in high school and at Center. He'd had a huge crush on Brooke in high school, but Brooke was dating someone else and wanted to be "just friends," breaking Tony's heart in the process.

Brooke asked, "Did he drop out of school?" He would've been scheduled to graduate this coming spring, same as Brooke.

Marie laughed. "Heck no. Near the top of his class and pre-law. He worked here last summer and is filling in during the break."

Tony looked their way. His eyes settled on Brooke. He raised an empty glass in her direction. She nodded in response. "Tell him thanks," she said.

"Will do," Marie said. "But I think he got the message." She winked before heading off to check on other customers.

The one thing about signing and lip-reading is that two people can have a conversation regardless of how much noise, or loud music, is surrounding them. The sisters took full advantage of this opportunity, "chatting" away while those around them were forced to sit in silence and listen to the music or get up and take a turn on the dance floor—which was why most of them had come to this nightclub: to dance!

But not Leah and Brooke, not this night. They had too much to catch up on. Leah shared news about finishing her third semester at Davidson. She told about her classes, having settled on a major

BARRIER ISLANDS

(Psychology), continuing her pursuit of ballet (her teacher wanted her to do a silent dance recital at the end of next semester but Leah wasn't quite ready to commit to that), and taking up a new hobby of coed Frisbee tag.

And boys? Brooke asked.

Leah smiled slyly. *I will never tell!*

Brooke made an exaggerated pout.

So Leah gave in. *O.K. I have lots of boy friends.*

Any one boyfriend?

Leah shrugged with feigned nonchalance. *Not today.*

Yesterday? Tomorrow?

Leah laughed (that sound again—so natural, even with the music, yet unexpected to Brooke). *You are nosy!*

With my sister, of course!

Leah nodded. *I miss that.*

Me too.

Leah reached across and took Brooke's near hand and squeezed it.

Brooke squeezed back. *But quit changing the subject!*

Where was I? Leah said.

You well know.

Oh—boyfriends! None at the moment.

Any favorites?

One or two, but they are my secret.

Cute?

What do you think?

Can they sign?

My lip reading has got very good.

How do you talk to them?

Write at first, then lip reading. A couple have learned to sign.

With you teaching them, of course.

Of course.

JEFFREY ANDERSON

Brooke had to marvel at how much Leah had grown up, and grown in confidence and resourcefulness, from the shy and reticent girl who first entered public school as a junior. That was the year Brooke had gone off to Center and wasn't home to help Leah or hold her hand. She recalled there were many crises that year—for Leah at home and Brooke in college (without Leah to limit her impulsiveness). But they'd somehow survived, and now look at her baby sister.

And you? Leah asked.

Putting milk in one end, cleaning up the result at the other.

Leah looked puzzled.

Brooke laughed. *Feeding Jodie and changing her diapers.*

She is so cute. Such a good baby.

I guess.

No?

She's wonderful. It's just a full-time job, that's all.

Onion?

He's a good father and helps change her diapers. But he works a lot and sometimes late.

His parents?

They would take Jodie and raise her if I let them.

Want to tell you how to do it?

Want to make Jodie theirs.

But she is theirs, partly.

She is mine, Leah, first and foremost.

Leah stared at her sister. What had become of the easy-going, break all the rules, live for the moment girl she'd always envied? What was binding her up now? *Shawnituck?*

It seemed so different from here, Leah—laid-back and free. I did not have to wear shoes if I did not feel like it, or a dress to dinner, or put on make-up if I went shopping.

Leah held her hand up. *You never wore make-up when you went shopping!*

BARRIER ISLANDS

And don't you know I heard about it!

Leah shrugged then nodded. Brooke had ruffled plenty of feathers in her day, within their family and among her classmates.

Brooke continued. *But it turns out Shawnituck has its own set of unwritten rules.*

Everywhere does.

Why didn't you tell me?

Leah stared a long moment at her sister, not sure how to answer this question. *I tried to. You would not listen.*

When?

When you visited me at school right after telling me you were pregnant.

What did you say?

I asked if you knew what you were doing.

And what did I say?

You told me what color you were going to paint the nursery and that your baby's name would be Jodie.

Brooke laughed, just now recalling the long weekend she had spent with Leah even before she'd told Onion of the baby started within her. *What color would I paint the nursery?*

Turquoise. She spelled the uncommon word on the table with her finger.

Brooke nodded. That had been her plan. But they didn't have a nursery. Jodie's crib was pushed into the corner of their common room. *I had it all figured out.*

Leah nodded slowly.

Just then an inebriated man neither of them knew came up to the table and reached his hand toward Leah. "I want to dance with you," he slurred.

Leah didn't shrink from his aggressive approach. She smiled serenely but shook her head.

"Come on. You're beautiful. I've got to dance with you."

Brooke said in a low growl, "She said 'no.'"

The guy looked toward Brooke with a scowl. "I didn't hear her say anything."

"She's deaf, asshole. She can't say anything."

He seemed momentarily caught off guard then rushed to recover. "That's O.K. We don't have to talk." He turned again to Leah. He pointed to her then to himself then to the dance floor. He reached out and grabbed her wrist that was resting on the table.

Brooke started to stand, not sure what she'd do but sure she had to do something.

Leah quickly caught her eye and gestured for her to stay put. Then she looked across the room to the big man seated on the stool beside the entrance. His name was Al, a former linebacker at Center and now bouncer for the club. He'd been watching the sequence and, with the glance from Leah, was off the stool and beside their table in a flash. He wedged himself alongside the drunk. "She doesn't want to dance," he said.

The guy looked up at Al, hesitated, then let go of Leah's wrist. "Sorry," he said petulantly. "I didn't know she was deaf. What the hell you let deaf people in here for anyway?" He did not wait for a response but walked across the dance floor, bumping into several dancers, before heading out the door.

Al turned to Leah and signed *Sorry for the disturbance.*

Leah nodded then glanced to Brooke. *This is my sister.*

Brooke extended her hand. "Brooke."

"I'm Al." He took her hand in his much larger one. "Nice to meet you. We love your sister."

"So I've seen."

He smiled. "She can really dance."

"So I've heard."

Leah gestured, *Not tonight.*

Al nodded then looked back to Brooke. "Nice to meet you."

"Likewise." She gazed unabashedly at him as he walked back to his seat by the door. She turned to Leah. *Another 'friend'?*

Leah shook her head. *Just a friend.*

He can sign.

Not my type.

Brooke looked across the room to where Al was sitting on his stool. He made a little wave when their eyes met. Brooke couldn't help but wonder what it would be like to be single again.

6

Brooke sat on her childhood bed in her childhood room with Jodie finally asleep on her lap. The baby had been a champ throughout the trip—handling the ferry crossing and long car ride and several days jammed with parties and other gatherings leading up to, including, and following Christmas. She'd been terrified by Mr. Nicholson dressed in his red suit and black boots and fake white beard (the designated Santa at the church Christmas social) but otherwise happily accepted the free and frequent passing of her body from one stranger eager to make her acquaintance to another, a skill she'd long since mastered on Shawnituck. But somewhere among all those pawing hands and slobbery kisses she'd picked up a virus. She started coughing last night and this morning woke with a runny nose and a low-grade fever. Momma wanted to take her Doctor Manning—the pediatrician that had treated her and Leah and Matt—but Brooke had resisted. On the island they didn't have a pediatrician, and Brooke had treated Jodie's two previous illnesses with a mix of over-the-counter medication, home cures, and lots of attention and care. She'd apply those same techniques here, for now anyway.

But earlier this afternoon, with Father at work and Momma out returning gifts and Leah at a matinee with friends, Brooke's adamant self-sufficiency had been sorely tested. Jodie would not stop crying no matter what she tried. She'd walked around the house and up and down the stairs what seemed a hundred times, bouncing Jodie on her shoulder or swinging her in the cradle of her arms. She'd rocked her in the rocking chair, snuggled her on the bed, tried cool cloths on her forehead, warm cloths on her stomach. Nothing worked. Jodie's tears and plaintive wails produced first frustration then fear within Brooke. What if she'd miscalculated this illness? What if her home care wasn't sufficient? What if Jodie had a serious illness that was already beyond control? She'd never confronted such a prospect, and now she was

BARRIER ISLANDS

having to face it alone. She had no car to drive somewhere if she had to, and no one to call to ask advice—Father was on the road for a sales meeting, and Momma and Leah beyond phone contact. She could try to reach Onion at the restaurant, but what would he do? She was alone in this crisis. And her fear and isolation grew with each scream from her inconsolable baby until she finally dissolved in tears herself, burying her face in Jodie's chest and sobbing uncontrollably.

She couldn't say when Jodie stopped crying for the deafening roar of her own sobs. Nor could she say how long she'd kept her face buried in Jodie's nightshirt, now damp with their mixed tears. When her sobs finally abated, all she heard was Jodie's beating heart. She lifted her head. The room had grown dark in early twilight, and the house was utterly still. But she could see Jodie clearly enough, stretched out on her lap, drawing hoarse sleeping breaths through her mouth as her nose was clogged. Brooke bushed Jodie's damp hair from her face then felt her forehead. It felt cool for the first time today. She took the corner of the blanket and wiped the tears from Jodie's cheeks and cleared away some of the mucous around her nose. Jodie scrunched up her face and Brooke gasped in fear the wailing would resume. But Jodie's eyes never opened and she rolled to one side and pushed her face into the cleft formed by Brooke's legs. Her breathing grew less labored, and her body relaxed against Brooke's legs. Slowly Brooke's body relaxed also, drained not only of fear but of all energy. She felt totally empty.

She thought of Momma from twenty years ago confronted with these same challenges and fears, possibly seated in this very spot with the baby Brooke asleep in her lap. How had she managed it? How had she raised three children and never once seemed confused or uncertain or frightened? Where had her strength come from and why couldn't her daughter summon it now? Bearing a child was one thing but having the skills to raise her quite another. The calm certainty that Brooke had so often rebelled against now seemed the very quality she needed—not to benefit herself but for Jodie, for her child's safety and well-being.

46   JEFFREY ANDERSON

But where could she find it in her thin reserves of self-control and equanimity? Those were Leah's traits. Brooke had none of that.

She heard a rustling and looked up. As in a dream she saw Leah, clad in a bulky dark sweatshirt and jeans and stockinged feet, walk across the carpeted floor and sit on the bed beside her. The mattress creaked slightly.

Leah glanced at the sleeping Jodie then focused her eyes on Brooke. She reached up and gently wiped away the trails of tears still left on her sister's cheeks. She smiled then signed *You will be O.K.*

Brooke sighed, a sound lost to all in the room, even herself. She signed back. *How?*

Leah considered that a minute then signed the only thing she knew. *Love will show you.*

Brooke thought but didn't say *That's not enough.* Then she rose, set Jodie in the crib Momma had borrowed, then headed to the bathroom down the hall to shower before dinner.

7

Daffy showed up around 8 with a box of presents under one arm and a bulging canvas tote slung over her other shoulder.

It was New Year's Eve, and Jodie and Brooke had got back late that afternoon after a trip that had begun in the pre-dawn winter dark at her parents' house. Onion had met them at the ferry and dutifully helped load their bags into his father's rusting pickup. He'd given the baby a long and passionate hug but hadn't touched Brooke or said a word during the short drive or while unloading the truck. After getting everything in the apartment, Onion had asked, "Coming to The Buffet?" He was referring to the restaurant's All-You-Can-Eat New Year's Eve Buffet. Just about everyone still on the island attended this annual affair, calling it Times Square on Shawnituck though it ended well before midnight. Jodie was frazzled and fussy and still recovering from her cold, and Brooke herself was more than worn out and now furious with her petulant husband. "Too tired," she said tersely before turning to get Jodie out of her tiny jacket and the pink stocking cap Momma had knit for her. When she stood up and looked, Onion was gone, off to work (she assumed) without another word. Brooke had changed Jodie's diaper, put her in her flannel footed pajamas, then nursed her and put her to bed. The apartment suddenly seemed very quiet and cold—till Daffy arrived.

Brooke grabbed the box and set it on the card table that doubled as their dining table. Daffy lowered the tote onto the kitchen counter.

"Not at The Buffet?" Brooke asked.

"Been to one, been to them all," Daffy replied.

"So I never have to go again?" she said with a raised eyebrow. She'd been to last year's and watched everyone else get a little tipsy—some more than a little—from the rum punch while she, then five months pregnant, sipped on club soda all night.

"That would be your decision—next year," Daffy said as she unpacked the tote bag. "This year, I brought The Buffet to us." She displayed plastic-wrapped bowls of fried chicken, fried flounder, French fries, hushpuppies, and slaw. She set a covered cake plate off to the side.

"Is that what I think it is?"

"If you think it's my fig cake!"

Brooke cheered and gave Daffy a high-five.

"But you still haven't seen the best part," Daffy said. From the bottom of the bag she pulled out a fifth of Jamaican rum and two quart jars filled with a pale-green mixer. "The heck with that weak punch—we can mix our own right here!" Though still too young to drink legally on the mainland, Daffy (like her brother and most other teens on the island) had been experimenting with alcohol and other recreational drugs for years.

While Brooke slowly rallied from her daze, Daffy grabbed two tall plastic cups off the open shelf, dropped in some ice cubes from the freezer, and combined a generous portion of rum with some of the mixer in each cup. She handed a cup to Brooke then tapped it with hers. "Happy New Year," she said.

"Happy New Year," Brooke replied and took a swallow of the drink. She grimaced. "Whew—one or two more like this and it really will be a 'happy' new year."

Daffy smiled. "That's the idea. " She took a sip of hers then asked, "How's Jodie?"

"Conked out." They both looked toward the crib at the far end of the room, where all that was visible was a shallow mound under several blankets.

"How'd she handle the trip?"

"Like a champ, though she picked up a cold halfway through. Still got some sniffles but the fever is gone."

"Best baby in the world!"

"Don't I know it."

Brooke took another long swallow of her drink then used its energizing pulse to bring her back to life. She stuck a Bee Gees tape in the portable cassette player and turned it up loud, then got out plates and silverware for their dinner as Daffy uncovered the bowls of food. They loaded those plates, sat at the card table, and gorged on the delicious fare while they sipped on their drinks and filled each other in on their Christmas activities. The Howards had set aside Brooke and Jodie's presents—and there were a lot of them, especially for Jodie—to be opened at a combination late-Christmas and New Year's Day party tomorrow afternoon at Miss Polly's.

"But I wanted you to open yours from me in private," Daffy said with a mischievous grin that made her pale face both disarming and strangely beautiful.

"Before or after fig cake?"

"After," Daffy said then took their near-empty cups to mix two more drinks while Brooke cleared their plates and got down bowls for the gooey cake.

A half hour later the girls sat on either end of the slightly tattered over-stuffed couch basking in the warm and soothing afterglow of the rich and heavy meal—perfectly crowned with Daffy's fig cake complemented with a generous scoop of Jan's (homemade on the island) vanilla ice cream on top—and now well into their third round of rum with a splash of mixer. Somewhere along the way Brooke had switched from the Bee Gees dance beat to the gentler rock of Fleetwood Mac with Stevie Nicks' haunting voice.

Brooke looked at Daffy and could not help but think of Leah. Her sister had driven them to the mainland's ferry dock and dropped them off only seven hours ago. They'd parted with hugs and tears and sign language vows—mostly through the eyes—to spend more time

JEFFREY ANDERSON

together in the coming year. Yet they both knew those pledges were empty. Leah was fully engaged in college and her blossoming life, and was not going to come out here to be a third wheel in her marriage; and Brooke couldn't show up a Leah's dorm with Jodie in tow, even if Onion would let her go (which, based on his behavior tonight, he never would).

So it was with a void in her heart, a void that had been there for several years but that she'd somehow dodged acknowledging let alone confronting, that she gazed on her sister-in-law. While both girls had long blond hair, and quiet and watchful natures (so different from herself), Leah was much more beautiful and graceful and (now) self-possessed. But that meant Brooke might help Daffy in a way no longer needed by Leah.

"So what do you hope your new year brings?" Brooke asked. She figured Daffy might think a minute before launching into a list of teenage fantasies—a boyfriend, a new surfboard (Daffy was the best surfer on the island), a functioning car, an "A" in history: the sorts of things Brooke had wished for when she was seventeen (oh so long ago!).

But Daffy grinned before looking at the floor. "Adulthood."

Brooke was startled. "And what is that?" Daffy would turn eighteen in the coming year, but somehow she doubted that's what she meant.

Daffy, still staring at the floor, said, "Freedom."

"From—?"

"Childhood."

Brooke held silent and waited.

Daffy looked up after a moment and held on Brooke's stare. "That's my life out here—the baby of the Howard clan. I'd hoped maybe Jodie's birth would help. She'd be the youngest. But it hasn't made any difference. I'm still Daffy, like the duck—the Howards' Little Ugly Duckling."

"Who do you want to be?"

"Anything but Daffy."

"Tell me."

She hesitated then blurted out, "I want to be Daphne. I want to be someone known and appreciated for who I am, not what family I come from, or the island."

Brooke, coming to the island from outside, had always seen it as an exotic place of adventure and freedom from her social world's rules and restrictions. She'd never contemplated what it would be like to be born and raised here. "I thought you liked being called Daffy."

"Did you ever ask?"

Brooke grimaced. "I'm sorry."

Daffy laughed. "Don't be sorry, Brooke. You were just following everyone else's lead. But don't ever assume a kid likes their designated role."

"Should I call you Daphne?"

Daffy smiled. "That would be nice. That's what Ralph calls me."

"Mr. Hopson?"

Daffy blushed. "Yes. Mr. Hopson."

"Then Daphne it is, Daphne."

She smiled. "But only between us for now. Don't want to shock the oldsters too bad." She jumped up. "Speaking of shocking—." She retrieved the box off the table, pulled out three neatly wrapped presents, and set them on the couch next to Brooke. "Time for you to open them!"

Brooke grinned. "I'm not sure what I think about the 'shocking' part. Nothing will explode in my face, will it?"

"Well—."

"Daffy!"

Daphne arched her eyebrows.

"I mean, Daphne!" Brooke corrected.

"No hazardous chemicals or explosives enclosed," she said then raised her hand. "Scout's honor."

"When were you ever in the scouts?"

"I saw it on T.V."

"Which should I open first?" The gifts were of three sizes—the smallest about the size of a pack of cigarettes, the second of a hardcover book, and the third of a shoebox.

"Smallest to biggest," Daphne said.

"Good things come in small packages?"

"Good things come in all packages," she said, then added, "I hope."

Brooke quickly opened the smallest gift. Inside the box that was inside the wrapping was a bracelet of tiny shells strung on nylon line. "It's beautiful, Daphne!" Brooke said as she slid it on her right wrist.

"I made it when I was fourteen, before I realized I wasn't a shell artist. But I've not known who to give it to, till now."

"I love it. Thank you for saving it for me."

Daphne grinned. "Next."

Brooke opened the middle-sized gift. It contained what looked to be an antique hinged frame with silver edging and a silver clasp holding the hinges closed. "This is gorgeous! Can I open it?"

Daphne nodded. "It's old, but it shouldn't fall apart."

Brooke gently undid the clasp and opened the two-sided frame. Inside were two photographs mounted beneath oval-shaped glass. The one on the left side was a profile of a horse's head against a brilliant blue sky—Daphne's wild horse captured in a moment of stillness on a beautiful island day. The right side held a photograph of a seated woman looking down on a sleeping baby in her lap—a Madonna with child. It took Brooke a second to realize that the Madonna was she, the child Jodie. Closer examination indicated that the photo was taken while she was sitting on a bench in the restaurant's alcove, sometime last summer when Jodie was just a few months old. Brooke marveled at how serene she looked, like someone else. For that matter, both photos exuded a tranquility that was extraordinary. Brooke looked up from the photos to the photographer. She started to speak but found her voice missing as tears rose to her eyes.

Daphne laughed. "That bad, huh?"

Brooke shook her head vehemently and managed to croak, "No, that beautiful."

"I got the frame from Dad's shop and polished it up. I don't know how old it is or where it came from."

"And the photos?" Brooke's voice returned as she blinked away the sudden tears.

"Both from last summer—two wild fillies caught in a moment of stillness!" She laughed. "Bet you didn't even know I shot you that day."

Brooke shook her head. "No idea."

"The best pictures are when people don't know they're being photographed."

"I bet you're good at that."

"Hiding in plain sight? Been doing it all my life. Just had to add the camera."

"Don't ever stop."

"Hiding in plain sight?"

"Documenting the world so beautifully."

"Open the last present," Daphne said, turning the topic away from herself.

Brooke carefully closed the frame and set it on the upright packing crate that doubled as an end table to the couch. She then tore into the wrapping of the third gift, somehow sensing that it didn't contain fragile contents (and hoping she was right). Inside was a plain cardboard shipping box with the white label addressed to Daphne Howard. The box was unopened and wrapped so well that Brooke had to get the scissors out of the kitchen drawer.

"The suspense builds," Daphne joked and began a low drumroll on her thighs.

54 JEFFREY ANDERSON

Brooke sat down on the couch and cut through the packing tape. Inside was another box. This one had *Trojan* printed on it, and *Contains One Gross (twelve boxes of twelve condoms) of Lubricated Latex Condoms with Reservoir Tip.* Taped to the box was a sheet of paper with the message: *Thank you for purchasing our product. Please enjoy!* It took Brooke a few seconds to realize that this was not a practical joke, that the box really contained what it claimed to contain, that her baby sister-in-law had given her a Christmas gift of one hundred and forty-four condoms. When that fact had settled in, she shrieked, "Do you think we have sex five times a day?"

"Why not? I would!" Daphne said, then quickly added, "If I had a partner and a place to do it."

"Sundays too?"

Daphne purred. "Sundays six times!"

"What about church?"

"After church, and before."

Brooke shook her head. "How did you know where to order them?"

"I'll never tell."

"Good. I guess I don't want to know too much about my little sis-in-law." Then she looked at the box of condoms and did a quick estimate of cost. "But this is way too much, Daphne. Let me pay for them."

"No way—my gift. That's what allowance is for! I'll think about you enjoying them," she said, then added, "But not in too much detail."

To that both girls shrieked, "Ewww!"

Brooke took the box and went into their bedroom and hid it far under their bed. Then she dug through one of her bags from the trip until she found a large metal-clasped manila envelope containing numerous documents and a thick catalogue. She returned to the living room and handed the envelope to Daphne. "It's not wrapped pretty, but this is your Christmas present from me."

BARRIER ISLANDS

Daphne undid the clasp and pulled out the contents. It was a complete admissions package from Center University, including a course catalogue. Brooke had visited Center's campus during her trip home and picked up the materials. Also in the packet were several typed letters of introduction to admission officers and deans, all extolling the many qualifications and desirable character traits of one Daphne Howard. The letters were signed by Brooke with the identifying phrase beneath the signature: *Brooke Fulcher, daughter of Franklin Fulcher.*

Daphne said, "I thought you said you wouldn't be a good reference."

"I exaggerated my bad behavior just a tad. Father and Momma graduated from Center, and so did my brother. And Father has several classmates who are now administrators there. These letters will get you in to meet them."

"How can I thank you?"

"No thanks required. These letters get you in the door. The rest is up to you."

Daphne paled, seemed to shrink into her old self.

So Brooke quickly added, "Just take them your transcript and a portfolio of your photos, Daphne. They'll throw open the doors and give you a scholarship to boot."

Daphne's countenance lightened a shade, but she still looked doubtful. "I'm just a shy girl from an island forgotten by time."

"You're a brilliant young woman and photographer with a unique background. I know these guys, Daphne. They are desperate for diversity. They'll take you in a minute."

"I'll hope you're right."

"I am. You'll love Center."

"Then why did you leave it?"

The question caught Brooke off-guard. She hesitated before saying, "Love."

JEFFREY ANDERSON

"Oh, yeah—five times a day."

Brooke laughed. "Maybe—a few times."

"And no condoms."

"Nope. Jodie instead."

"Your wish back then was the same as mine."

"How so?"

"You wanted adulthood—and got it."

Brooke nodded slowly. "I guess so. Be careful what you wish for."

"No. Wish for what you wish for, then grab it when it comes along."

"And live with the results?"

"Nothing else to do."

From outside the walls of the apartment there arose the crackle of fireworks. Brooke checked her watch—11:30. Where was Onion? The buffet had ended hours ago.

Daphne also looked at her watch. "I'm going to the fireworks." The island's volunteer fire department set off fireworks over the harbor every New Year's Eve and Fourth of July. "Want to come?"

Just then, Jodie rolled over in her crib and whimpered, perhaps stirred by the firecrackers outside, or the shrieks of the girls.

Brooke shook her head. "No thanks—adulthood calls!"

"So it does." Daphne leaned over and hugged her sister-in-law. "You're such a good mother. You're such a good friend. Thank you."

Brooke said, "My little sis."

"Always."

Jodie cried out again. The two sisters parted, Daphne to put on her coat and head out into the night, Brooke to lift her daughter out of the crib and nurse her.

8

Onion turned on the light and sat heavily on the edge of the bed.

Brooke rolled over and glanced at the digital clock—3:47. She was instantly awake and surprisingly clear-headed despite the several rounds of Daphne's potent punch. "Where have you been?"

"What do you care?" Onion said, his voice thick, his words slightly slurred.

"I care where my husband has been when he comes home at 3:47 in the morning."

"Why? You don't care about him at any other time."

"Cut the crap, Onion. Where were you?"

"I went to Jack's and watched the fireworks. That's what you do on New Year's Eve."

"With your wife at home?"

"Your choice, not mine."

"We've got a baby, remember?"

"She could have stayed with Mom."

"Jodie was exhausted and so was I."

"Not too tired to party with Daffy."

"Daffy was nice enough to keep me company. More than I can say for her brother!"

"Your choice, not mine."

"What was my choice?"

"To leave me alone on Christmas."

"What's that got to do with tonight?"

"Got everything to do with tonight," Onion said, his voice rising. "You take my daughter away on her first Christmas, don't care about me or my family."

"Jodie and I are with you and your family every day. But she has two sets of grandparents, and I took her to see the other set for a few days."

"Left me!"

"I asked you to come! I wanted you to come!"

"Leave on Christmas?"

"It's not that hard, Onion. I did it last year. You could've done it this year. My family wanted you to come."

"They don't care about me."

"You're my husband. You're Jodie's father. They care about you because we care about you. They want to get to know you."

"Have them come out here."

"They will, but not on Christmas. Kids go to their parents on Christmas."

"See!"

"What?"

"Kids stay with their parents."

"You can't be in two places. We alternate."

"No!"

"Yes!"

"You said we'd never spend a night apart!"

"And so did you!"

Onion stood and ran out of the bedroom and slammed the door to the outside. The apartment was suddenly eerily quiet. Brooke held her breath, waiting for Jodie to start crying. But she didn't. Then Brooke had a sudden panic and jumped out of bed. She ran to Jodie's crib and was immensely relieved to see her baby sleeping on her stomach, her legs pulled up under her body, her butt raised beneath the blankets. She picked Jodie up and carried her into their bedroom and laid her in the middle of the bed. Jodie emitted a couple of faint squeaks but never opened her eyes. Brooke climbed in beside her daughter, pulled the covers over the two of them, reached across Onion's side, and turned off the light.

9

The day after New Year's dawned clear and cold.

After breakfast Brooke bundled Jodie in her ski jacket and knit cap and carried her the few yards to her in-laws house then unbundled her to leave her with Lil. Just yesterday, at the combined New Year's Day and Brooke-Jodie Christmas at Miss Polly's, Jodie had suddenly decided to start crawling. And, once started, she wouldn't stop. She'd crawled all around Miss Polly's living room, then around their apartment last night, and now was crawling around Lil's den this morning. She couldn't get enough crawling. While Brooke was amazed and delighted to see this development in her daughter, she was also anxious that Jodie would crawl somewhere she shouldn't go or get into something she shouldn't get into. This mobile Jodie was a new adventure and responsibility. She was reluctant to leave Jodie but also felt, after almost two weeks of near constant attention to her baby, the need for some time apart. And she trusted Lil as a careful and attentive babysitter. She grabbed Jodie in mid-crawl, gave her a hug and a kiss, then set her in Lil's lap.

"Don't let her out of your sight, please," she said to her mother-in-law.

Lil laughed. "Are you kidding?"

Brooke shrugged. "Sorry. This crawling stuff has me freaked out."

"Get used to it. Only gets worse."

"That's what I'm afraid of."

Once outside Brooke cut through the back yards of several neighbors (all members of the extended Howard clan), followed a narrow road of planks laid across the sand to the one paved road on the island, crossed that road and climbed over several tall dunes, then descended the final dune to the ocean and the long stretch of Park Service beach that ran to the northern tip of the island. The shoreline was empty far as she could see. For the first mile or so, there was one set

60   JEFFREY ANDERSON

of tracks just below last night's high-water line—probably Mutt Erwin out at dawn to check for salvage—then those tracks turned inland and left her utterly alone. In the old days and even as recently as last fall, such stark emptiness would have unnerved Brooke. She'd always needed people—partly as audience, partly as assurance—however much she chafed at some of their rules and hypocrisies. But recently she'd begun to crave small doses of solitude, preferably outdoors, away from the reminders of commitment and obligation. Today especially she felt such an urge, and now breathed in the cold and pristine air and soaked in the seemingly infinite expanse of water and white shoreline.

Yesterday's party had gone smoothly enough. Onion had appeared late in the morning to shower and change. He'd not said a word about the previous night, and she chose not to bring it up. The words they exchanged were all carefully selected to be neutral, and mostly focused on which presents went to which clan member. Brooke meticulously wrapped each gift and included ribbon accents and flourishes of curly-cues and hearts on the labels. At the party, the large crowd was jovial if a little muted in the wake of all the recent celebrations. There were only a few references to Brooke and the baby's absence over Christmas, and these were all gushingly diplomatic—"We so missed you last week!" and "Santa arrived looking for little Jodie and had to take all those presents back to the North Pole" to which someone added "With poor Rudolph crying all the way!" to which Samuel, Jodie's six-year-old cousin, asked "Is that why his nose is red?" to gales of laughter.

Brooke kept a smile pasted on her face the entire time, and was enthusiastically thankful for their many gifts—genuinely so in several instances. But she couldn't shake a feeling of claustrophobia, no doubt instigated by the too warm and too crowded house. She hardly saw her husband, as he spent most of his time outside on the porch or in the converted garage playing pool. When she did see him, as when he was summoned to sit beside her on the couch and help open the

BARRIER ISLANDS

presents given to both of them, she felt a mix of anger and hurt. She still wondered where he'd been before he came home last night, and where he'd gone when he'd stormed out; but she didn't dare broach the subject—certainly not here, maybe not ever. Daphne could provide some clues, or maybe outright answers to these questions; but she made a conscious choice not to put her sister-in-law in the middle of their marital tensions. All of these bottled up emotions had fed into Brooke's craving for solitude and wide-open spaces.

And that craving was fulfilled here beside the ocean. She walked quickly and resolutely along the firm sand just above the lapping waves. A stiff and cold north wind blew directly into her face, sometimes carrying with it a peppering dose of sand, other times a saltwater spray. She hunkered her face down into the upturned collar of her canvas field coat (a Christmas gift from Leah) yet was secretly glad for this assault of nature as it distracted her from more painful and complex contemplations. She felt that if the shoreline was indeed as infinite as it looked, she would never stop walking, never return to the close nest and net that held her so tightly.

But the shoreline didn't go on forever, not this one nor any. This particular stretch ended some miles out at the tip of the island where a channel of deep and fast-moving water marked the sound's exit into the sea. Across the channel, the mainland was brightly visible, seemed almost close enough to touch in the brittle air though it was in fact a mile away beyond choppy and treacherous water. No boats were out in this channel, now or ever, as the shifting shoals and violent cross currents made it impossible to navigate. Sometimes diehard surf casters worked these waters for their rich mix of sport fish, but none today. There was a lone figure just this side of the island-end's parking turnout, walking back and forth with a plastic pail and a short-handled rake over a stretch of freshly exposed beach. Brooke identified the figure as her Aunt Greta from her slate-gray lobsterman's hat and matching calf-high rubber boots, working her favorite stretch of beach for shells and driftwood. At first she'd resented the sight of another human on this day but had a change of heart when she identified her. She'd seen Greta at her grandparents' house the day after Christmas for the annual Fulcher holiday reunion. She'd seemed unusually quiet and withdrawn that day, and Brooke had never caught her alone to try to find out why. So her frown was replaced by a grin as she approached from behind, her aunt bent over and gently raking back some broken shells to see what lay beneath.

Brooke was only a few feet away when her aunt turned suddenly and yelled, "Stop!" She thrust her rake forward like a weapon.

Brooke jumped back. "Jeez, Greta! I'm not a thief."

Greta's menacing glare held unbroken. "Only thieves and misfits out on a day cold as this!"

"What about you?"

"Misfit from Day One!" Her scowl eased yet still she held out her rake, its sharp and sand-scoured tines glinting in the sun.

Brooke held up her hands. "Then me too—misfit, that is. No thief!"

"You sure?"

Brooke hesitated a moment to try to determine Greta's meaning but gave up. "Only a giving heart," she said, more earnest than she expected.

"That's your curse," Greta said.

Brooke took one stride toward giving her aunt a hug but was again halted by the rake. "Greta!"

Greta smiled finally. "Hold your horses, deary." She let the rake fall to the sand then tilted its handle away from her. The action unearthed a near-flawless sand dollar that had been invisible to Brooke's glance. Greta gently tapped the rake against the ground to let bits of sand fall away then dropped the sand dollar off the rake and into her pail in a flash. "Now give me that hug," Greta said. "But no kisses—picked up this scratchy throat from Andy."

BARRIER ISLANDS

Brooke closed the few feet between them and leaned over for an awkward hug around the rake and bucket and lobsterman's cap. She noticed her aunt had a scarf wrapped around her head and neck, and a bulky sweater beneath her windbreaker. "Happy New Year," she said as she stood upright.

"They say it is," Greta replied. "We'll have to see."

"We can hope."

"We can."

They stood together looking over the channel until a particularly fierce gust of wind blew sand and salt spray into their eyes, which in turn triggered a coughing fit in Greta. Once her coughing subsided, Brooke shouted over the wind, "Lovely day!"

Greta said, "It is except for this damn wind. You want to warm up in the jeep?"

Brooke nodded and followed her aunt to the parking lot between the dunes and the old Army-surplus jeep sitting there like the scarred remains from a lost battle. Though the wind whistled through the cracks between the doors and the canvas top, the interior was much quieter and well-warmed by the sun's captured rays. They breathed audible sighs as Brooke latched her door against its bucking with the wind. Greta pulled off her lobsterman's hat but left the scarf pulled over her hair.

Attired like that and with her weathered and creased face fully lit by the sun, she looked almost ancient to her niece who was more used to seeing her as young and of boundless enthusiasm and energy. When had she turned old? "I'm sorry I didn't get to talk to you at Mim and Pap's," she said.

Greta shrugged. "I see you all the time. They don't."

"But we've got to maintain a united front—islanders against the world!"

Greta scoffed. "You fit right in with them."

"Of course—been there every year of my life, except last year."

"I never fit."

"I know. That's why you always fascinated me."

"And now you know the truth."

"What truth?"

"That I'm a lonely outcast."

"Greta!"

"I am. And I need to apologize to you."

"For what?"

"For bringing you here."

"I was dying to come!"

Greta held up her hand to still her niece, then softly confessed what had been troubling her since before Brooke and Onion had got married. "I needed you, see?"

Brooke shook her head. No, she didn't 'see.' Greta was, and had always been, the most self-sufficient person she'd ever known.

Greta chuckled and shook her head. "Fooled you like all the rest. I followed Andy out here the summer after he graduated like some lost puppy. He let me know in every gentle way he could that I shouldn't have come, but I came anyway. Then he let me know in a very hard way the folly of my choice by getting engaged to Barb. That should have done it, right?—sent me back to the mainland and school, maybe with my tail between my legs but still with a chance at a future.

"But I refused to leave. I told myself I was a martyr to love, wanting to be as close to Andy as possible even if he wouldn't publicly acknowledge his love for me. But I knew there was more to the choice than just some romantic idealism lifted from a fairy tale. I'd been quietly rebelling against Mom and Mary far back as I could remember and decided to use the excuse of love to make a complete break. A better balanced and more mature soul would have found a less radical way to express independence, but who ever said I was well-adjusted or mature?"

BARRIER ISLANDS

She paused and laughed then continued. "But it wasn't enough for me to crash my life. As the months turned into years, I needed affirmation of my choice, a vindication of my paltry life. It wasn't loneliness that haunted me. For some reason, I've never felt lonely; and Andy and I found ways to get together soon enough. But what I missed was approval, the very thing I'd rebelled against.

"And that's where you came in. I saw in you my rebelliousness, and so did Mary. And in her full sight, I gradually presented to you a view of my life and of this island that would appeal to that rebelliousness."

"But you loved it out here!" Brooke exclaimed.

Greta laughed. "With you watching, I could almost convince myself that I did."

"The paintings, the driftwood frames, the shell necklaces!"

"Mysteries from another world."

"Yes!"

"Yes."

"A lie?"

"Let's call it a one-sided presentation."

"Why are you telling me this now?"

"For Jodie. I don't want you perpetuating the myth to her. Fate blessed me by not giving me a child." She paused and reconsidered. "Or maybe not. Maybe a child would have forced me to see my life for what it was."

"And that is?"

"A coward's escape. Mom and Mary were tough, and I don't agree with their heavy-handed methods. But I see now they were mainly trying to point me toward a life with real opportunity, chances to go along with the responsibilities. I just didn't wait long enough to discover them."

"You still can. You're hardly forty."

"Forty-two in mainland years but good as a hundred out here—stuck in my island identity beyond changing."

"No, Greta!"

"Yes, Brooke." She leaned over and kissed her niece on the forehead then leaned back and sighed. "Maybe it is a happy new year after all."

Brooke stared at her aunt a long time before whispering, "Yeah, maybe."

Greta donned a big smile and said, "If you wait here for me to get my gear, I'll drive you back to town and heat up a pot of my chowder for lunch."

Without looking up, Brooke shook her head. "No, thanks. I'll walk back—could use the air."

Greta recognized the tactic but chose not to fight it. "Plenty of air out there today."

"Yeah, one thing we have in spades." Brooke opened the door and clenched the handle to keep the door from being wrenched from her hand by the wind. Standing beside the Jeep, she glanced around at what suddenly seemed an unfamiliar world. It was literally unfamiliar—the parking turnout bordered on three sides by low dunes. But somehow the strangeness extended beyond the immediate environs, hung over the whole island and its encircling blue boundaries—a new stark and brittle encampment. She turned and leaned into the vehicle. "Take care of that cold."

Greta laughed. "Thanks. Forgot for a minute I had it. Borrowed some of your youthful vigor."

"Keep it," Brooke said. "I'll make more."

"I don't doubt that."

Brooke started toward the village, pointed south, the sun in her face and the wind at her back. But instead of climbing the near dune and returning to walk along the ocean, she exited the turnout on the hard asphalt and walked along the lonely two-lane road that cut through the dunes. She told herself it was to minimize the wind and give herself a change of venue, but in fact at that moment she was terrified of the prospect of confronting the sea, its limitless blue sweep

BARRIER ISLANDS

67

with the solitary set of tracks along its edge. On the pavement she would leave no tracks nor be confronted with infinity. There was some reassurance in those restrictions, though the black line of road did blur in the distance into a haze of wind-blown sand and glare.

She was a good way into the trek when she heard a vehicle approaching from behind. She resolved not to turn or leave the pavement. The car could go around. She figured it was Greta and didn't want to encourage another invitation to lunch, one she might not find the strength to decline. She'd wave without looking up as the vehicle passed and continue on her solitary walk.

But the vehicle slowed as it passed then stopped a few feet in front of her, forcing her to look up. It wasn't Greta's Jeep but a shiny white pickup sitting high in the air on big tires. There were several tall surf-casting poles in pipes between the bed and the cab, the lures and leaders at their tips sparkling in the sun. Brooke immediately recognized the truck as belonging to Dave Weldon, a distant cousin of Onion's who had a fishing boat he hired out to tourists in season. During the winter he kept busy as a mechanic—boats and trucks—and did a little lobstering on the side when his late-night carousing and frequent bed-hopping didn't have him pre-engaged. She and Dave had had an alcohol-fueled one-nighter shortly after she'd arrived on the island, well before she'd settled on Onion as her permanent and lone partner. Ever since, she'd returned Dave's unabashed stares with a kind of amused but forthright "hands off" gaze of her own, though lately she'd taken to avoiding his glances and his presence as much as possible.

The passenger door of the truck swung open as she approached. She'd have to swerve into the soft sand of the shoulder to pass. Instead, she walked up and stopped at the open door.

"Get in," Dave said. He patted the vinyl seat that was at her chest height. "I'll give you a ride back to town." His eyes sparkled like the lures on his poles. His grin was disarming.

"That all you're offering?" she asked with a voice from a distant past.

He didn't miss a beat, reached through the open sliding rear window and between the poles and patted the white top to the blue cooler in the bed. "Have a few full ones left."

"They cold?"

Dave laughed long and hard.

Brooke climbed into the cab using the chrome foot step and handle. The door closed behind with a solid thud. A Boz Scaggs song she used to sway to at Center was playing on the radio. Dave popped the top on a beer and handed it to her, then cracked one for himself. They sat for a few seconds sipping the near frozen liquid and staring ahead at the windswept road with its small drifts of sand gathered in the lees.

"So where to?" Dave asked in a low purr.

"Driver's choice," she said, her voice gently rising.

Still he didn't put the truck in gear. Its big motor idled beneath their feet. "What you doing way out here on a day cold as this?" he asked.

"Walking. You?"

He laughed. "Fishing."

"Any luck?"

"No. Too cold for fish."

"Yeah. For humans too."

He shifted into gear and let out the clutch but kept the transmission in first, leaving the truck creeping along at only a few miles per hour, holding his beer can and the wheel with his left hand, his right hand cradling the shift knob. "By the way, Happy New Year," he said.

"Likewise."

Without looking toward her, his hand floated from the shift knob and came to rest on her knee. She looked down at that hand jutting out from the frayed and stained cuff of his beige canvas coat, the hand's skin weathered and still tan despite the season. When had she last seen a hand look like this? Almost imperceptibly to them both, she flared her left leg toward the gear shift, causing his unmoving hand to slide up her jean-covered thigh.

The truck came astride a beach turnout locals called "The Black Hole" because, unlike the other three along the highway, this one was not paved and regularly swallowed tourists' cars in its soft sand despite signs warning "Beach Vehicles Only." Dave's truck, its hubs locked in four-wheel-drive, easily navigated over the narrow access lane to the dune-shielded and empty parking area beyond. He switched off the truck's engine, set his beer on the dash, set her beer beside it then climbed atop her on the wide seat as she leaned back against the passenger door. As she stared at the white and round dome light beyond his shoulder she giggled at the thought of the one hundred forty-four condoms under her bed at the apartment and not a single one available to her now. Dave solved that problem by reaching under the seat and pulling out a foil-wrapped packet. She grabbed the packet, tore it open, and one-handedly unrolled the latex sheath over its destination with a practiced ease from some former life.

10

That night Brooke and her husband finally lay down in the same bed at the same time for the first time in two weeks. Jodie was sound asleep in the next room, clearly exhausted from her active day at Lil's and still more crawling about the apartment. Brooke had not realized just how dirty their unfinished pine floor was until she saw Jodie's hands and the stains on the knees of her Muppets pajamas. She resolved to scrub the floor tomorrow.

But now she lay on her back in their narrow bed with Onion beside her. The lights were out but the room was lit with the glow of the full moon and Lil's yard light pouring through the unshaded window. The room was cold, the heat from the woodstove in the main room not reaching quite this far back. Brooke pulled the patchwork-quilt bedspread tight to her chin, thought of pulling it over her head for warmth but figured that might give Onion the wrong idea—of prohibition or, maybe worse, of playful invitation. So she kept the covers at her chin and stared at the far-off ceiling.

Onion sat a little higher in the bed, his head and bare shoulders outside the covers, raised slightly on the pillow wedged against the wooden headboard. His breathing was silent, a clear sign to Brooke that he was not asleep or anywhere near it. His sleeping breaths were accompanied by childish yips and quiet groans that Brooke used to feel were charming but now found annoying, especially last year when they kept her awake after rising to feed Jodie in the middle of the night and returning to try to get back to sleep.

But there was only silence now as each stared into the dark and contemplated this return to their shared bed after the suspension of their promise never to sleep apart. Brooke thought about the other bed she'd slept in while away—her childhood twin bed with the soft mattress and the white painted metal headboard with its brass caps and accents. It had been so welcoming and natural on her return. What about the beds Onion had slept in while she was away? Was it only this bed and his childhood bed, in his boyhood room not twenty yards from where they lay? Or had there been another bed, one night or several? She wondered.

Onion rolled toward her onto his side and extended one arm across her body to her shoulder, pushing the covers aside, his hand caressing her neck then slowly up toward her face and hair. It was a gesture both gentle and familiar—the first step in a sequence that would culminate in an old sharing, their best common ground, that would also be somehow new, to the year at least, and maybe to their future lives.

"Is there a daycare on the island?" she asked in a firm whisper.

Onion's hand froze where her neck merged into her skull, just beneath her left ear. "A what?"

"A daycare—to watch over young children."

Onion's body slid back to its former location on his side of the bed and against the headboard. "They go to school during the day."

"But before kindergarten."

"Their mothers take care of them."

"And if their mothers are busy?"

"Then their grandmothers or aunts or older sisters."

"But if the mother is busy two or three days a week, that would be a lot to ask."

"Who's busy two or three days a week?"

"I might be."

"Why?"

"I'm thinking of going back to school. Part-time."

"There's no college out here."

"At Coastal."

"That's on the mainland."

"I know where Coastal is."

"How are you going to go to school on the mainland?"

"Part-time—two classes or maybe three. I could try to get them all on Tuesdays and Thursdays, but might have to do Monday, Wednesday, and Friday."

"What are you talking about?"

"Take the early ferry in, go to class, take the late ferry back out. It's a long day but I think I could manage."

"Why?"

"To get my degree."

"For what?"

"I don't know. To use it to get a job."

"Jobs out here don't require degrees."

"In case we move."

"We're not moving."

"Just in case."

"Why would we move?"

"I don't know—for Jodie."

"What about Jodie?"

"To give her more chances."

"Chances for what?"

"Life."

"This island has all the life she'll ever need."

"We can't be beach bums forever, Onion."

"We're not beach bums. We're married with a child."

"Living in your parents' garage, you working for tips."

"I could manage the restaurant one day."

"Yeah, divided among about a dozen of your kin."

"A good living."

"What about me?"

"You take care of Jodie."

"I can't just sit here forever. I'll go crazy."

"We can always use another waitress."

Brooke scoffed.

"What? You were good at it, always brought in the biggest tips." He laughed as his mind returned to an earlier attention. "Just flash that smile and shake that booty and watch the tips flow on in." He reached under the covers and pinched her butt through her flannel pajamas.

"My point exactly!"

"What point?"

She growled in disgust, rolled to her side, her back to her husband, and pulled the covers over her head.

Onion slid under the covers too. "We can pretend we're camping in the tent on the beach. Remember that?"

"Leave me alone. Go to sleep."

He found the elastic waist of her pajama bottoms and slid them to her knees.

She stopped resisting but didn't roll over to face him. In truth she was happy to hide their tension beneath a more primitive urge and consolation. Even so, she still remembered to reach under the bed. She slid the condom on without facing him or lifting the covers. He was startled but didn't protest, content enough with attaining after long pause his elusive goal—the panting and moans that rose quickly followed by genuine rest for both.

11

They settled into the rhythms that had defined their lives prior to the disruptions of holiday plans and demands. Brooke followed no particular schedule. She spent some afternoons at the restaurant, with Jodie confined in the foldaway playpen in the sunny entry, doing off-season maintenance tasks—painting, dusting, polishing the brass—for nominal wages between the lunch and dinner hours. Other days she'd do her shopping at the general store while carrying Jodie on her hip, always pausing to gossip with the "girls" (most of them twice her age or more) gathered around the toiletries counter or flirting with the "guys" (all old enough to be her grandfather) seated around the potbelly stove. Everyone loved the gregarious Brooke and fawned over the generally cheerful Jodie, one of the few infants currently on the island and the only one of Howard lineage and its associate public persona.

But unlike last summer and fall, when she was caught up with caring for and showing off her newborn, and last winter and spring, when the fatigue and back pain from her pregnancy kept her largely indoors and preoccupied with a cast of well-meaning visitors, this winter Brooke began seeking, and finding, solitary time, leaving Jodie with the ever-willing Lil. On clear days, she'd spend this time walking, sometimes in town (having to fend off frequent invitations to coffee or "island tea"—a shot of rum in warm lemonade) but usually on the uninhabited end of the island, never tiring of the ocean-side expanses and finding on the marshy sound-side quiet nooks to explore. She even ventured into the wild horses' mix of thicket and clearing, and once got almost close enough to Daphne's Ruby to brush her nose before the filly snorted and cantered off.

On the frequent wet days, with their numbing mix of fog, drizzle, rain, and sometimes wet snow, she started going to the school library, which was open to residents as well as students. She occasionally

BARRIER ISLANDS

checked out contemporary novels to read at home, but mostly she borrowed textbooks on computer science (a new field of study) and calculus (her specialty at Center) that could only be used in the library. Against all prior training and inclination and as a complete surprise, she took pleasure in reading the dense and dry textbooks, taking notes and doing the exercises in a spiral-bound, multi-subject notebook. When Daphne stopped by during one of the school's recess periods (for all grades) and saw the fat texts Brooke was reading, she called her "Einstette" to which Brooke asked "Meaning 'little' or 'feminine'?" and Daphne replied "Both" and Brooke said "Thanks, I guess."

When she'd first mentioned to Onion the idea of going part-time to Coastal, it was an impulsive suggestion born of a vague unease. It was her way of alerting her husband—or affirming to him: he'd already been alerted—to the existence of new needs and hopes for her life and theirs. But further reflection indicated that such a plan was—well, a virtual impossibility. First of all, the two-hour ferry trip each way would be grueling even if the water was calm, which it rarely was in the winter. Then there would be the challenge of getting from the ferry dock to Coastal's campus thirty miles away, another forty-five minute car ride minimum, assuming she could get someone to take her or borrow a vehicle from the island and pay the added ferry charges each way (though she could probably save money by leaving the car at the mainland's ferry station, if she could find someone willing to give her indefinite use of their car and risk having it vandalized at the unguarded parking lot). Finally, as she confirmed with a phone call the next day, registration for spring semester was already closed, and in any case transferring her credits from Center would require reapplying and being accepted to the university system, as her one-year leave of absence had expired last summer and she'd had to officially withdraw.

For some reason these obstacles to her near-term enrollment didn't curtail her planning. They only encouraged it, at least in her own mind, which was where the idea remained for some time. In her mind, she realized that going to school while living on the island would be too great a burden for everyone. Furthermore, the idea of returning to school part-time seemed unnecessarily tedious and slow. Why take four or five years to finish two years of school? She should just go back full-time and get her degree.

That is, if she could afford the time and the money to go full-time, and if she could get reaccepted into the university, and if she could live somewhere close enough to one of the campuses to keep the commute manageable, and if she could find someone to take care of her child nearly full-time, and if she could convince her husband to leave the place that he'd never left except for doctor's visits. Yet all these ifs only deepened her commitment to find a way, presented the sort of seemingly insurmountable obstacles that had, once upon a time not so long ago, been Brooke's favorite brand of challenge.

One night a few weeks into the new year, Onion came home in the early evening, one of his two nights a week not working the dinner shift. He carried with him a paper sack holding foil-wrapped fried flounder and hushpuppies left over from lunch along with a paper cup full of fresh-made slaw and a paper bowl containing two servings of peach cobbler.

"A couple beers to drink and some ice cream for the cobbler and you have a complete dinner," he said proudly as he unpacked the bag on the kitchen table.

Though Brooke had planned a meal of spaghetti and already started the sauce, she summoned a broad smile and said, "All my favorites." She pushed the pot of sauce off the burner before hugging her husband from behind and kissing his neck.

"Bringing home the bacon!"

"And don't forget the cobbler!"

"Never," he said.

BARRIER ISLANDS

Jodie was already in her high-chair at the table, making idle designs with the Cheerios on her tray and watching her parents in a moment of happy cavorting.

Brooke quickly laid out two place settings, opened a jar of baby food for Jodie and two bottles of beer, then sat opposite her husband at the table. He looked at her with that innocence of hope and expectation that had charmed her from their first meeting. She wondered where that look had gone these past months, or if it had been there all along and she'd simply missed it.

"We should bless the food," he said.

Brooke shrugged. Blessing the food was a habit reserved for large gatherings and special occasions, but she wasn't opposed. "Bless away."

He nodded and folded his hands and closed his eyes, but before starting he opened one eye a crack and saw Brooke grinning indulgently at him. "No peeking!"

Brooke laughed. "That isn't much of a blessing."

"No peeking during the blessing, or it won't take."

"Won't take us where?"

"Brooke!"

"Okay, okay. My eyes are closed. Let the calling forth of the Spirit commence."

"Brooke!"

Jodie said, "Book!"

Brooke giggled but kept her eyes shut and her voice still. She did reach out and clutch Jodie's tiny hand without looking.

Onion said quietly and reverently, "Dear God, let this food make us whole in your image and in your sight. Please keep our family happy and healthy, this night and always. Amen."

"Amen," Brooke said.

"Men!" Jodie shrieked and slapped her tray, making the Cheerios bounce.

"My thoughts exactly," Brooke said, leaving the subject of agreement—her daughter or her husband or both—ambiguous.

Onion, who'd kept his eyes closed for a moment as if in silent prayer beyond the spoken one, opened them now and with a glowing countenance announced, "Let's eat!"

"Meat!" Jodie said, though her dinner was split pea soup in a jar.

Halfway through the meal, Onion said, "I've got some news."

"What?"

"I've been accepted by the Coast Guard for seaman's training."

Brooke was stunned. "When did you apply?"

"Last week."

"And you've heard already?"

"Uncle Berg is the station commander, Brooke, and Dotty's his secretary. Let's say they gave me the inside track."

"That's great! I didn't know you were interested in Seaman's School."

"It was always my goal as a kid and in high school. Then this mainland girl came along and started waiting tables in the restaurant, and I kind of forgot about everything else."

"Mean old waitress."

"Beautiful young waitress—and wife and mother of my child."

Brooke stared at him and felt a void open in her stomach but said nothing.

Onion continued. "But that same girl reminded me of the importance of having goals greater than running a restaurant. So the next day I got the application and turned it in."

Brooke reached across the table and brushed his cheek. "I'm so proud of you, and so excited."

Onion blushed but managed to hold her gaze. "Thanks."

"So when do you start?"

"Well, I haven't officially accepted. I wanted to talk to you first, and of course Miss Polly. But if I accept, the next class starts in the spring."

"You've got to accept."

"Yes, I think so."

"And when do we move?"

"Move where?"

"To a Coast Guard training center." Brooke had known several Coast Guard recruits, all of whom had gone to training school for at least six months.

"That's the best part—we don't have to move! Uncle Berg will oversee the training here, at the station and on the launch. He said I might have to take the final written test on the mainland, but that would require only a day away. I would never have applied if we'd had to move."

"Why not?"

"This is my home, Brooke."

"Not even for six months or a year?"

"No way! It's crazy out there."

"Out where?"

"The mainland. The city."

"And me?"

"You came out here. You said you never wanted to leave."

"And Jodie?" Brooke said, nearly a whisper.

"She's a Howard. She'll grow up here same as all the Howards."

"Then what?"

"Then what?" Onion repeated.

"For Jodie."

"When she's grown she can choose what she wants—same as me, same as you. And she'll choose to stay here, with her family."

Brooke stared down at what was left of the dried out fish on her plate.

Onion stood and walked the two steps to the fridge. "Beer?" he asked.

Brooke nodded without looking up.

Jodie said, "Ear!" and pointed to the side of her head, mimicking the new word and gesture Brooke had taught her just that morning.

12

After seeing Greta the day after New Year's, Brooke didn't see her for several weeks. She'd heard at the General Store that she was sick in bed with a bad case of the flu but was declining all offers of care under a self-imposed quarantine. *Won't be responsible for infecting the entire island* was what the note stapled to her door read when Brooke knocked several times but got no response. She thought briefly of pushing the door open—surely it wasn't locked—but finally decided to grant Greta her privacy and isolation. She left the container of home-made chicken soup in front of the door with her own hand-scribbled note: *Get better now! Love, Brooke.* She wished she could call her aunt on the phone to check on her, but Greta had never had phone lines—"Mainland malarkey!"—installed to her cottage. So Brooke left her soup and hoped for the best.

And apparently it worked—her soup or Greta's obstinate independence or both—as Brooke glimpsed Greta with Andy on a blustery Sunday checking out some of the ice-coated sand sculptures at Winterfest, a recently instituted weekend festival designed to break up the monotony of winter and try to bring in a little tourist income in the off season. Brooke wanted to run up and give her aunt a hug but shied away from disturbing her time with Andy, or raising the ire of Miss Polly by publicly acknowledging and endorsing their "adulterous relationship." She resolved to visit her aunt early in the following week.

But then Lil was sick the following week and Brooke had no babysitter for several days. She could have taken Jodie with her to Greta's but was suddenly fearful of Jodie coming down with the flu and no doctor or pediatrician available on the island. She'd never thought of the island's lack of resident medical care before. The school nurse, a woman in her sixties who kept her pills in hand-labelled hand-blown glass bottles from the nineteenth century, was the closest thing they had to such care. But now, with everyone around her, or so it seemed,

82   JEFFREY ANDERSON

sick or recovering from illness, Jodie suddenly seemed dangerously vulnerable. Brooke thought of asking Daphne to babysit for an hour or two after school, but her sister-in-law was unusually scarce, working on a special project for school. So Brooke stayed in with Jodie all that week and, truth be told, forgot about her plan to go see Greta.

Then Greta disappeared again and no one knew why. The girls at the General Store speculated, in whispers and knowing nods, that she might be shacked up with Andy, though someone else said Andy was on the mainland at a duck-decoy show. Others said she was doing her "art thing"—immersed in a burst of creative inspiration where she would cover her windows with easel paper and not emerge for days at a time. But no one really knew what Greta was up to, or cared much beyond the gossip. After twenty years on the island, she was still an outsider.

So the following Tuesday, a gray fog-bound day that never brightened beyond dawn's glimmer, Brooke managed to pin down Daphne and get her to sit with Jodie while she went to visit her aunt. As she walked through the back yards and sodden paths on the way to Greta's, everything appeared different. Wind-shaped and stunted live oaks extended their branches like ghost arms out of the fog; low fences rose up like traps, vehicles loomed as sleeping giants. Brooke tried to shrug off the eerie images as the result of her overactive imagination, but a profound sense of foreboding settled over her as she neared Greta's cottage.

The foreboding only deepened when she reached the cottage and saw no lights shining through the windows. The place looked as deserted as one of the numerous rentals on the island closed down for the winter. Maybe Greta had gone with Andy to the decoy show. Brooke wondered if the windows were covered with easel paper, blocking the light. But a closer look revealed the windows weren't covered, let her see into the seemingly deserted kitchen and living room. She knocked once on the door, then again, then again, each

BARRIER ISLANDS

83

knock becoming progressively louder and more desperate. She tried the knob. The door was locked—not the knob but some inside latch. When had Greta installed that?

Brooke walked the four strides to the door off the porch, the one that opened directly into Greta's bedroom. It was solid wood. There was a window to the left of the door, but it had a shade pulled low. Brooke took a deep breath and tried the knob. The door creaked open.

"Greta?" she whispered.

No response.

She pushed the door further open. "Greta?" she said, her voice only slightly firmer.

The room beyond the door was darker than the dark day. It took a moment for Brooke's eyes to adjust to the thin light. Eventually she could discern some of the details of the small room. There was a dresser with a mirror above glowing silver on the wall. There was a wooden arm chair beside the dresser and a pile of clothes on the floor. Brooke took one step into the room and looked behind the door. Her eyes had acclimated sufficiently to allow her to make out the small twin bed wedged between the door and the corner of the room. At first she thought the bed empty. Then came a low groan and a movement on the bed. Brooke nearly jumped out of her skin.

Then she set to action. She closed the door behind her, ran to the side of the bed, stooped down and found the switch to the bedside lamp. The room suddenly leapt forward in what seemed a brilliant light. Huddled under many layers of covers but so slight as to hardly raise them in the least was Greta. Her cheeks and eyes were sunken, her skin a deathly gray, and her far-spaced breaths a hoarse rattle.

"Greta! Greta!" Brooke said in what sounded like a shot to her but was hardly above a desperate whisper. "Greta, it's Brooke."

Greta's head rolled toward Brooke but her eyes didn't open.

"Greta, what's the matter? Wake up!"

84   JEFFREY ANDERSON

Greta groaned again and moved her arms weakly under the covers but still didn't open her eyes.

Brooke then realized the house was freezing. Greta had electric baseboard heat but mainly heated with the woodstove to save money. Apparently neither heat source was on. Through the cold, she smelled a sharp odor and identified it as stale urine. Had Greta soiled her bed linens?

Brooke panicked then. She jumped up and ran toward the living room. She tripped over a plastic dish pan, spilling the liquid it held, the source of the odor. Brooke grabbed some clothes off the pile by the dresser and wiped up the spill best she could in the dim light. Then she ran into the living room, turned on the overhead light, and checked the woodstove. It was full of cold ashes, with no paper or firewood in the box to the side. She'd have to bring wood in from outside but didn't have time. She went back into the bedroom and found the control to the baseboard heater and turned it all the way up. Within a few seconds the metal of the heater began to click as it warmed. It would take a while to heat the room, but it was a start.

She knelt again beside the bed. Greta's head was thrown back on the pillow and unmoving. Only the intermittent rattling of her breaths indicated she was alive at all. Brooke needed help and needed it fast but had no idea how to get it. She looked about wildly for the phone she knew wasn't there then screamed at the top of her lungs. "Where's the damn phone!"

She reached down to check the heater. It was warming steadily. She quickly checked to make sure there was no paper or clothing that might ignite if it got too hot. The heater was clear. Still, the room was freezing.

Brooke leaned over the bed and put her face just inches from her aunt's. "I'm going to get help," she said slowly and firmly. "I will be back as quick as I can." She started to say, "Don't you die on me" but couldn't bring herself to say the word, not aloud or even in her mind. The phrase

BARRIER ISLANDS

ended at "Don't you—." She ran out the side door and slammed it in her wake.

Though nothing on the island was truly remote, Greta's converted fishing shack was as remote as any year-round residence. It sat at the end of a narrow sand track, several hundred yards beyond any other cottages or packed dirt roads. In the deepening dusk and the still denser fog, Brooke could hardly find her way, had to stare down at the tire tracks (from whenever Greta last drove her Jeep) to keep from wandering off into the dunes or thickets. Worse, Brooke really didn't know where to go to find help. She could follow her earlier tracks back to Bridge and Lil's, but that wasn't the nearest house. She could try knocking at the cottages along this drive, but they were all seasonal and almost certainly empty. She would be wasting precious minutes pounding on doors to vacant houses without phone service even if someone were there.

She finally decided to head for the main road and the small community center with its combination police and fire departments. They also had shortwave radio links to emergency services on the mainland. After several minutes of fast-paced walking, keeping an eye to the ground, she broke into a trot then a flat out run, no longer able to watch the ground but trusting her instincts to keep her in the track.

Then she hit a pothole. She fell face first into a thick layer of slimy muck, knocking the wind out of her. The ground was soft and she wasn't seriously hurt, but the sudden shock of the earth opening beneath her mixed with the dark and the mud and the fog nearly paralyzed her. This was an unfamiliar and dangerous world, even the ground a threat. How could she move forward?

But then she thought of Greta, alone and dying in that shack. She pulled herself out of the pothole, wiped the mud from her face and hands, and pushed on, no longer running but walking as fast as she could while keeping an eye on the ground. When she reached the paved road, she turned south and started running.

JEFFREY ANDERSON

The community center was one of the first buildings on the highway as you came into town, just past the gas station and bait shop, both closed at this hour. A light glowed from the center and she ran up to the double doors at the entry. Thanks God one was unlocked. She burst into the small waiting room with the one desk in the corner. No one was there. There were halls leading off to the left and the right, one to the fire marshal, one to the police department. She ran to the left, to the police.

Halfway down the hall was an open door with a light streaming out. She turned the corner and ran straight into Alton Powell, the only fulltime paid police officer in town, a barrel-chested, big-voiced man with a shock of unruly white hair above his quick smile.

Alton was at first startled but then laughed aloud as Brooke crashed into his chest. "What you been doing, Brooke—mud wrestling?"

"Greta! She's sick. We need help."

Alton grew serious. "What's wrong with Greta?"

"I went to see her. She didn't answer the door. I went inside and found her in the bed. She couldn't talk. She could hardly move!"

For a jovial easy-going lifelong islander, Alton could hustle when he had to. He grabbed his hat and his truck keys and was down the hall in a flash. He used the radio at the dispatcher's desk to alert the Coast Guard at the ferry station of a "possible medical emergency," concluding the transmission with, "standby for further instructions." Then he was out the door and to his four-wheel-drive off-road truck.

Without a word, Brooke followed and climbed into the passenger seat. In the truck's dome light, she noticed that the backs of her hands and coat sleeves were smeared in drying dark mud.

Despite the fog, Alton drove very fast over the paved road and down Greta's drive, the truck swerving from side to side in the soft and wet sand. Brooke didn't know whether to be terrified or relieved at

BARRIER ISLANDS

Alton's obvious urgency. She finally closed her eyes and surrendered to his lead. Greta would finally have help.

Inside the cottage, Greta was still breathing, though barely—and with that awful thin rattle coming out of her chest, unlike anything Brooke had ever heard.

Alton took one look, said "Stay with her," then ran out to his truck to use its radio to call for more help.

Brooke sat beside the bed holding Greta's cool hand. She whispered, "Let her live." She noticed then that the room was considerably warmer than earlier, no longer felt like a tomb. She looked to Greta's ashen face. "I won't leave again," she said.

But less than fifteen minutes later she was forced to renege on that promise as too many people tried to cram into the too small room. Each new visitor exuded a sense of island authority and proprietorship that ignored Brooke's blood and emotional attachment to the patient. First came the fire marshal then the school nurse then the apothecary's pharmacist then a coast guardsman with emergency medical training. Each newcomer gently but firmly pushed Brooke farther and farther from the bed until she was pressed against the wall between the dresser and the door. At first the sight of these attendants filled Brooke with hope that an intervention, any intervention, to reverse Greta's condition was at hand. But as each visitor arrived, checked the patient, shook his or her head, and mumbled words unintelligible to Brooke but clear in their grave tone, she grew ever more impatient and furious.

Finally, with a half dozen hulking figures each still in their damp coats and rain gear arrayed around the bed and staring down in silence at the gasping figure, Brooke screamed from behind, "Don't just stand there—do something!"

Alton, who was by then at the end of the line of attendants and closest to Brooke, turned to her and put his arm around her waist and eased her toward the door to the living room. Brooke tried to resist but was no match for his weight and girth and inexorable will. When he'd pushed her into the living room, she looked up and saw that the large room was full of islanders—many Howards, including Miss Polly, but also non-family members and a few faces she didn't recognize. Where had they all come from? And as she entered the room, the low murmur of the crowd, which she just now became aware of, suddenly hushed and everyone turned to stare at her.

Brooke burst into tears, blindly forced her way through the crowd and out the front door and onto the equally crowded front porch and beyond that out into the yard that was jammed with vehicles and bright as day with all the headlights blazing. She stumbled past silhouettes of bodies and around the fenders and bumpers of the four-wheel-drive trucks and past the corner of the cottage. There she finally found darkness, or the closest thing to it in this place at this moment and fell to her knees on the wet soft ground and sobbed.

Alton knelt beside her, put his arm over her heaving shoulders, and waited for the worst of her sobs to subside. "Brooke, the pneumonia has progressed too far."

Brooke turned toward him. Despite the fog and the dark, she could see his face clearly in some light of unknown origin. His eyes were the kindest and most sympathetic she'd ever seen. "Can't you get her to a hospital, with real doctors and real medicine?"

Alton shook his head.

"Why not?"

"This fog has everything shut down, Brooke. Normally we could bring in a medi-vac and have her to a hospital in under an hour, but not tonight. Nothing's moving—no choppers or planes. Even the ferry is suspended. If I thought it would help, I'd take her myself in the skiff; but she wouldn't make it, and maybe I wouldn't either."

Brooke stared at him for the longest time. She couldn't grasp how someone so young could be allowed to just die, how all of modern medicine could be so powerless in this place at this moment. Her eyes said all this, but her voice said nothing.

BARRIER ISLANDS

"We needed to know about this several days ago, when we would have still had a chance."

She jumped up and ran into the deeper dark of the back yard, where it merged into dunes.

Alton stood upright slowly on stiff knees. He considered following her but decided not to. He turned back to his responsibilities to the patient and the island residents that now surrounded her.

When Brooke reached the dunes, she turned to her right and walked parallel to them until she found the opening to the water marked by a narrow boardwalk that became a dock extending out into the water invisible below. She walked without hesitation out onto the dock, directed by memory of her many visits at all times of day or night her first summer out here. Back then her concerns had been self-centered—at first loneliness for Leah, then confusion about some early love interests and crushes, then in a swoon over Onion, and often to clear her head of intoxicants before passing under Greta's sharp eyes.

But tonight she had no thoughts for herself. At first she thought only of Greta, that her torment end soon and as painlessly as possible. She whispered aloud, "I'm sorry I wasn't here sooner" and somehow knew her aunt heard. From the end of the dock she could hear the water lapping against the pilings. She wondered how it would feel closing around her. At first it would be cold but soon not so much. Quickly numbness would take away all the shock and pain.

Then she remembered Jodie. How could she have forgotten? Her worldly responsibilities didn't end with Greta. They'd barely begun. *For Jodie* Greta had said in their last conversation in the Jeep parked at the end of the island. That's all that mattered now.

She found her way back to the cottage, her way lit by the light of all those headlights glowing in the fog. The smell of wood smoke was thick in the air. Someone had lit a fire in the woodstove. The cottage would be stifling by now. She emerged from the dark into the circle of light. Lil and Bridge were standing there beside Alton's truck.

"Jodie?" Brooke asked Lil.

"Daphne's got her at the apartment, long as need be."

Brooke nodded. She turned toward the cottage.

"Onion's on his way," Lil said behind her.

Brooke walked up the steps. As she entered the porch, the crowd gathered there silently parted. She considered taking the shortcut to the bedroom through the side door off the porch, but it was blocked by Miss Polly and her niece Barb, Andy's wife. Brooke continued straight through the front door and the kitchen and the living room. The islanders grew silent, stepped back. Just before entering the bedroom she spotted Andy's white hair and beard in the back of the crowd, somewhere near the woodstove. She paused and waved for him to join her, but his face disappeared. Had she imagined it?

She walked into the bedroom. Those wedged in there pressed to the side, making a narrow path to the bed. Greta was lying there, same as before—her gray face framed by the pillow, her body hardly raising the bedcovers. Brooke stepped forward and touched her hand on the covers. It was only after standing beside the bed for maybe minutes or longer that Brooke realized the awful rattling breaths emanating from the shrunken shell of a body had ceased.

13

Snow Whitaker, the island's funeral director and taxidermist, provided body prep and embalming services for free in return for Brooke's purchase (using Momma and Father's credit card number) of a fine mahogany casket. He laid Greta's small body attired in the one dress Brooke could find in her closet, a short-sleeved beige linen button-up that she'd worn to Brooke's wedding under her canvas field coat, in the big casket and invited Brooke to come view his handiwork in the formal front room of his nineteenth century house. Brooke declined the offer, saying she would view the body along with her family at the church on the mainland. She instructed Snow to give Andy a chance to see Greta, but he said Andy never answered his calls.

Snow arranged with a mainland funeral home to have a hearse sent out on the ferry. On the bright and surprisingly warm morning of the first day of February, Onion and Bridge and a couple cousins recruited from the restaurant carried the casket out of Snow's house and across the wide front porch and slid it into the back of the hearse on the metal rollers. The hearse's driver, a young man named Smithfield Bowles with slicked-back black hair and a thin mustache, locked the casket down using the built-in metal clamps then added two securing straps "in case the crossing got rough."

Brooke, in a dark navy dress with a white lace collar she'd borrowed from Daphne, nodded, set her overnight bag on the middle of the front seat, and slid into the passenger side for the short ride to the ferry dock. As Smithfield guided the bulky black station wagon through the village center, residents lined both sides of the street to watch them pass. Men dressed in all manner of work clothes—fishmonger's aprons and boots, carpenter's belts and jeans—doffed ball caps and knit stocking caps. Women looked down in respect, a few shedding silent tears, blinking against the glare. The older kids were in school on this weekday, but a few younger children gathered and stared. One waved, another saluted as they passed. It seemed like a dream to Brooke. The faces, almost all of whom she knew by first name, appeared a cast of strangers there beyond the windshield. She shivered slightly though the car was warm with the heater running and the sun pouring in.

Onion had offered to come with her for the funeral, but she had responded without a moment's reflection, "No. You stay and watch Jodie." She thought the decision was for his benefit. She knew he didn't want to come and wouldn't force him into an uncomfortable situation. But part of the choice was for herself. She wanted this final farewell to be for her mainland family, for Greta's mainland family that was, ultimately and finally, her only family.

Her decision to leave Jodie was similarly spontaneous but of complex subconscious origins. She'd never been away from Jodie overnight, and would have to spend one night on the mainland before returning the next day. But she didn't want to precipitate a fight with Onion over taking Jodie to her family again, so soon after the Christmas trip. And she couldn't imagine grieving in front of Jodie, confusing her daughter with the inevitable tears and sobs. Unlike the happy gatherings of just over a month ago, this sad duty must be out of sight of her daughter.

Once the ferry had cleared the harbor and was well into the crossing route, both she and Smithfield got out of the car to get some fresh air. The wind was brisker out here on the water but still not cold despite the time of year. Smithfield pulled out a pack of cigarettes and lit one. He extended the pack to Brooke. She shook her head. He tried to engage in some small talk between puffs on his cigarette, but Brooke barely responded with single-syllable answers. Finally he said, "Guess you want to be alone."

She nodded. "You don't need to watch over me."

He sauntered down the deck. There weren't many on the ferry this morning, but there was one young woman with long blond hair travelling in a pale green VW Beetle. She was throwing some potato

BARRIER ISLANDS 93

chips to the gulls trailing the ferry. Smithfield walked up to her. Brooke wondered if he'd make much headway dressed in his black suit and white shirt with the burgundy necktie. For some unknown reason, she hoped he did. She hoped the girl would invite him back to her car, maybe share a joint with him or engage in some innocent pawing fun.

Brooke looked down at the gray-green water swirling past the rusting flanks of the ferry. She recalled looking down at this same water from this same spot of deck rail headed in the opposite direction more than a year and a half ago. It was cold and blustery that day in May, and all the other passengers were either in their cars or the lounge. But she walked out to the railing and stayed there for the two-hour trip, breathing in the salt air and a new freedom. She was going to meet Greta to begin her summer adventure on the island. She had no idea what she'd find out there, but she knew it would be exciting. She somehow knew it would change her life.

Now she was pointed toward the mainland with her aunt's body safely encased in the coffin tightly strapped down in the black hearse. She'd never seen a hearse on the ferry before. It seemed at odds with all the surrounding life and racket—the gulls screeching, the diesel engines roaring, the water lapping, the sun shining, Smithfield chatting up the blond girl. The hearse appeared as a black hole in the midst of all this life.

But where was she in this picture? She rarely tried to take an eagle's eye view of her life. The very thought of such a perspective terrified her. How could her actual life live up to any of her hopes and expectations? But Greta's presence, in her heart more than in the coffin, wouldn't let her dodge the question. Where did she fit in this picture? Was she the girl at the stern, feeding the gulls, flirting with the overdressed guy? Or was she the somber niece transporting her wayward aunt's body back to her shocked family, to her final resting place in the ground? What were her duties? What were her responsibilities to the world, to family, to herself?

And to Jodie, a voice that seemed to originate simultaneously from inside and outside her head said loud enough to rise above the racket surrounding her.

"And to Jodie," she repeated, with lips and voice in a low whisper. Her own needs, now and far as she could see into her future, were a dense quagmire of impulsive desires, contrarian ideals, and grudging disappointments. How could she sort through that? But her daughter's needs going forward were simple: safety, sustenance, and opportunity. That was something she could commit her life to, a clarity of purpose that would give meaning and direction to her jumbled life.

And love? the voice asked.

"That's part of everything else," Brooke whispered, meaning for Jodie.

Is it? the voice asked.

But this last was lost beneath a long foghorn blast from the ferry's bridge, marking the approach of land. Brooke looked around quickly, as if waked from a trance. She walked to the side of the hearse and climbed into the passenger's seat. Where was Smithfield? she wondered, suddenly impatient to be on their way, though docking and auto release was still ten minutes or more into the future.

Smithfield emerged from the VW Beetle a few minutes later, straightened his tie, slicked his hair into place, and took his seat behind the steering wheel, once again focused on delivering his charge and his cargo to the church and the family and friends waiting there.

14

Momma's hometown was a farm village in the midst of the broad coastal plain. "Nothin' but soybeans and small talk," Grandpa would say rocking on his front porch looking out over the endless fields—brown in the winter and early spring, green from late spring through fall. The white clapboard Methodist church anchored one quadrant of the crossroads that marked the center of the village, with a fellowship hall connected to the worship space by a covered breezeway and the fenced cemetery beyond that.

Brooke's immediate family—Momma and Father, Leah and their older brother Matt taking a break from grad school—were there and waiting when the hearse drove up promptly at one in the afternoon. Her grandparents, aunts and uncles from both sides of the family, and most of the village's residents were also there, many of the women busy in the fellowship hall's kitchen preparing for the reception to follow the two o'clock funeral, the men out smoking in small groups in the dirt parking lot or wandering individually around the cemetery in the bright sun. Though Greta had forsaken her hometown decades ago, no one here had forgotten her; and they'd turned out today in force—to welcome her back, set her in her final resting place, and support her parents and each other through this eons-old but always new trial.

Father and Matt and six other designated uncles and cousins carried the coffin from the hearse into the dim parlor off the sanctuary. There, and with only the family present, Grant Errington, owner of the local funeral home, opened the casket for the private viewing. Brooke noticed a slight wince of censure pass over Mr. Errington's face as he raised the lid and looked in at the contents. Brooke, carefully wedged between Momma and Leah, glanced into the coffin once the lid was all the way raised and Mr. Errington stepped to one side.

Greta's body was well-situated in the white velvet lining of the coffin, her hands neatly folded at her waist, the beige dress all ironed

96   JEFFREY ANDERSON

and buttoned up. Her eyes and mouth were closed, and her short gray-flecked brown hair carefully combed and held in place with a thick glaze of hair spray. But her face retained the grayish cast from those awful last hours, and her cheeks were sunken in. For that matter, her whole body was sunken in, seemed as if there was little more than air beneath the dress's linen folds. Brooke could hear again the rattle that had emanated from that body. She shuddered involuntarily. Momma gasped then burst into a sob. Leah to Brooke's right and Father to Momma's left remained strong and held the other two against collapse. Brooke recovered enough to look beyond the head of the coffin. There sat Grandma in her wheelchair with Grandpa immediately behind, holding onto the chair's handles. Their faces were unflinching and inscrutable.

Mr. Errington closed and sealed the coffin before nodding to Smithfield to open the parlor doors to allow guests in to greet the family and offer condolences. Brooke stood in the receiving line and shook each person's hand and quietly thanked them for coming. Most just said they were sorry for the loss. A few asked after Jodie and congratulated her on the birth. None mentioned Onion or Shawnituck.

A short while later the family filed into the dim lofty sanctuary behind the coffin on its rolling bier. Somehow Brooke got stuck at the far end of the family's front pew, with Leah next to her, then Matt, Momma, Father, and Grandma and Grandpa. She briefly wondered if this seat of estrangement was somehow intentional. But this fret quickly passed as Leah's hand found hers and held it tightly throughout the service even as her sister's eyes and face stayed pointed forward, in a show of dignity and reserve or in an attempt to keep from dissolving into tears. Either way, Brooke clung to Leah's hand through the vaguely familiar hymns and the round-faced preacher's measured eulogy—"Greta was a passionate free spirit who chose to go her own way"—and the prayers and commendation, that hand her anchor not only in the service and today's storm but also to her family and past.

And still she held that hand in the brittle sun and biting wind beside the yawning hole exposing dark, sandy soil in the fence-bound cemetery behind the church. In past visits here—her grandparents' 50th anniversary in the church's fellowship hall, Uncle Blake's wedding—Brooke had always thought the cemetery's fence was to keep animals and wayward children out. But today as they lowered the coffin into that black hole, she wondered if the fence wasn't really intended to keep wandering souls in, or at least imply as much. Wherever Greta strayed in this life, she was here, at home with her kin, for eternity. Somehow the thought both troubled and consoled her, and how mixed up was that?

At the close of the brief graveside service, Reverend Stovall extended a worn shovel toward Grandpa for the casting of the first spade-full of dirt onto the sunk coffin's top. Grandpa released the handles of Grandma's wheelchair and took the shovel in his creased and bony hand but only long enough to thrust it, handle first, at Brooke. That wooden handle seemed a long finger of accusation, and she involuntarily recoiled from the attack. What had she done to deserve this? But Leah held her in place and, after a few seconds' pause, stepped forward with her to take the shovel. When Brooke still refused, Leah released Brooke's hand and signed to her sister—*For us, and for Greta*, ending with her hand half-open at her heart, holding them all at her heart. But who was holding whom? It didn't matter. Leah's signing, pointed at and understood by only Brooke, gave her the strength to take the shovel, push it deep into the soft dirt beside the hole, and toss the dark sandy soil into the yawning void. It struck the coffin's lid with a sound that echoed through everyone gathered—everyone, that is, except Leah, who felt only her sister's sadness echoing through her soul.

15

Brooke sat on the edge of the narrow twin bed with Leah beside her. Leah was in a full-length flannel nightgown, well-prepared against the chill. Brooke was in sweatpants and a long-sleeved t-shirt—as usual, somehow less appropriately attired than her sister, though this time it seemed to matter more. But why? Who would know or care, other than Brooke herself?

They were in the second guestroom of Grandma and Grandpa's house, the small one at the end of the upstairs hall, tucked up under the sloping gable roof. Momma and Father were in the other guestroom, the larger one equipped with a double bed, Momma's old room. This was Greta's room growing up, and this Greta's bed, though the old sagging mattress had been replaced some years ago. As schoolgirls visiting for the annual Rankin reunion the day after Christmas, Brooke and Leah would retreat with Greta to this room, sprawl on this bed to hear stories of how Greta would sneak out over the porch roof outside the one small window to meet some high-school jock waiting at the end of the drive in his souped up pick-up, or be told more recent tales of Greta's new home, the exotic island caught between the mainland and the endless great ocean, a world unto itself. Shaw-ni-*tuck*, Greta would say, always putting the accent on the last syllable to give the word and the place it represented more force and imperative (as if it needed it). Greta would tell Brooke these stories, and Brooke would "translate" for Leah, signing rapidly and adding numerous dramatic flourishes with her expressions and gestures.

Sitting silent and motionless on the edge of Greta's childhood bed, Brooke realized that it was during these story sharings that she unconsciously adopted Shawnituck as her destination and her destiny, and that that decision grew not only out of Greta's rapt tales but also somehow out of her signing to Leah, that she took an investment and ownership in the place through passing it on to Leah. And how much

BARRIER ISLANDS

of that force of ownership had she carried out to the island with her on that first and only fateful visit to Greta? How much had the place and its inhabitants, one in particular, become her destiny because she had chosen that it would be so all those years earlier, relaying Greta's stories to Leah on this very bed?

Following the bountiful reception, as they were picking up some trays of chicken and dumplings for their dinner tonight, Momma had caught Brooke alone for just a minute and made her only verbal reference to her deceased sister. "Don't end up like her!" she said in an adamant whisper. Brooke had wanted to ask what exactly she meant, but had been stopped by the approach of one of the church ladies with a coconut cake in a carrier for the family's dessert. And she'd not found Momma alone in the busy hours since.

Nor at this point did she really want to. She knew what Momma thought she meant—to not end up dying alone on a remote island of a curable disease. Or is that all she meant? Maybe she also meant to not forsake family, friends, and the society that had raised you in favor of people who in the end would not be there when you needed them. But where did that place Brooke, Greta's one proximate family member, absent when she needed her most? How much of this tragedy was her doing, her failure to be who she was supposed to be?

And what about Jodie? She'd avoided thinking about her all day, to protect herself from how much she missed her daughter but also from how much she owed her, the full extent of her responsibility to make the right choices for her daughter. Greta had made that obligation crystal clear in their last conversation. She'd suppressed the force of Greta's warning in the weeks since but couldn't quiet the words now. *For Jodie!* But *what* for Jodie? *Don't end up like me!* And where would Jodie be if she did?

She turned to her sister. Leah was staring straight ahead into the dimly lit chill of the room. She had a serene look on her face, as if seeing or sensing something in the still room that gave her calm assurance.

But what in this day or this setting could do that, give her that repose? She desperately needed Leah to tell her but wouldn't startle Leah with a sudden request. Instead, she approached her sister as she often did through their childhood—by gently touching the notch at her elbow, covered with pink flannel this night, then following her forearm down to the exposed wrist and lightly brushing the soft flesh of that inner wrist with her fingertips—their old game of tickle-flesh.

Leah was not surprised by the contact and for several minutes kept staring ahead—immersed in Brooke's gentle touch and the memories it summoned. Leah's eyes drifted shut. This was not Brooke's intent; but she'd not force the issue, briefly glad to be able to give someone ease on this sad day.

Leah withdrew her arm from under Brooke's hand, then turned and faced her sister from less than a foot away. She signed, *You will know what to do.*

Brooke looked puzzled. She'd not asked any question.

Leah smiled. *About Jodie. About your life.*

Brooke raised her eyebrows in a simple but adamant question—*How?* How to decide? How to implement her decision?

Leah weighed Brooke's question. She knew the weeks since Christmas had been traumatic for Brooke; and even at Christmas she'd seemed ill-at-ease, far from the confident person who had chosen Shawnituck then chosen, wooed, and married Onion. Though Leah had been on the periphery of Brooke's life since her move to Shawnituck, eighteen years of prior near-constant companionship had left her in touch with Brooke in ways that transcended distance and separation. Brooke was still Brooke, beneath this new life she'd donned. She needed only to find her way back to that center. *Find your heart again and follow it.*

That is what got me here.

Leah laughed. *That is O.K.*

Greta is dead. Onion will not move. I am trapped.

Leah turned from Brooke. She stood and began canvassing the room, looking in the empty drawers of the old dresser, checking out the closet smelling of mothballs, finally looking under the bed. She ended in front of Brooke, kneeling on the pallet of blankets and a sleeping bag that would be her bed for the night while Brooke slept on the twin. From there she laid her arms on Brooke's knees then slowly trailed her hand over Brooke's torso to end at a spot at the center of Brooke's chest. She pressed her fingers against her sister's breastbone. She didn't have to sign her meaning. Her eyes and hand carried all the message that needed to be conveyed, that needed sharing the end of this sad day.

16

Onion rose above her in the dark. It wasn't true dark. There was the nightlight she kept on just outside their cracked bedroom door in case Jodie stirred and she had to find her way to the crib without tripping over something. And there was the yard light Lil and Bridge burned all night at who knows what expense to ward off intruders or maybe wandering ghosts from the cemetery down the lane. So it wasn't completely dark, but dark enough to somewhat mask what they were doing under the sheets if anyone were to peak in the window, though the grunts and moans they were exchanging would surely give it away if the movements under the bedcovers didn't, and those sounds would easily penetrate the former garage's thin and uninsulated walls and would also drift past the open bedroom door and possibly wake Jodie—hell, lift the roof and wake the whole island if Onion didn't drop the decibel level a bit.

She pulled her free hand from beneath the sheets and gently brushed his parted lips with one finger. He quieted a tad but didn't slow his determined march toward their oldest and best sharing. It did feel good, she couldn't deny that; and the condom made him last longer, another plus.

But now that she was outside herself, she couldn't get back inside her body, at least not completely. So instead she studied her husband from down in the shadows of the pillows and the covers. His pale face seemed luminous, lit by some hidden light. His eyes were shut, his head thrown back as if getting ready to howl (she sure hoped not!) or maybe in prayer—but to whom or what? His hair glistened with sweat though the room was cool. The muscles in his neck were taut cords. She tried to find in this snapshot the boy she'd fallen in love with, seduced, and married. She tried to recall what had brought her here—to this boy, this family, this apartment, this bed. But try as she might, she couldn't find that feeling, couldn't find that love or that attraction or that memory. This failure did not produce fear or anxiety or revulsion or even emptiness in her. She liked this posture, this pursuit, this person doing what he was doing, this bed and the permissions it granted. Oh, yes, she liked that—and the frenzy of desire his actions were indicating, the crescendo they were rising toward.

Those efforts brought her back into her body—a little at first then a little more and a little more then completely. She was swallowed by the need. Her quieting fingers became claws in his back. Her measured breaths turned into pants, her sheathed teeth into nips, gentle bites and pulling lips. Yes, yes.

Had she retained any vestige of perspective, Brooke would have seen close-up just how potent and imperative this level of sharing was, how it could and did dictate decisions, actions, whole lives far into the future—years, decades, generations.

But she missed that truth in the blaze. And later, when she woke deeper in the night with Onion asleep atop her, she noticed not his weight or the smell of pot on his breath or his damp hair on her cheek. All she could feel was the copious wetness dripping from her core and the touch of skin, not latex, where his penis still rested inside her.

17

Daphne tapped on the door one night when Onion was working the dinner shift. Brooke was bouncing Jodie on her knee while seated at the table, trying to tire her daughter so she'd finally go to sleep. Since Jodie had started crawling, she seemed to have unlimited energy and curiosity, was endlessly getting into stuff left on the floor, had just today pulled the trash can over on herself. Fortunately it was plastic and not heavy, but the clatter and the scattering of beer cans and food wrappers had frightened them both. You'd have thought that lesson would have slowed the toddler; but not a half hour later she'd pulled the cooler lid shut on her fingers as Brooke unpacked some fish Bridge had brought by for their dinner and the freezer. Jodie was into everything and beginning to accumulate the nicks and scars of her adventures—a crooked left pinky finger from somehow dropping the crib side on her hand (Crab Howard, the island's resident homeopathic healer, had assured her it would grow out straight; but Brooke wasn't so sure) and a small scar over her right eye from somehow sliding out of her highchair. Everybody else seemed to think these the requisite marks of normal childhood; but every time Brooke looked at them she felt guilty, somehow negligent in her one responsibility in life—Jodie wasn't yet a year old and already scarred forever!

"You know it's open," Brooke yelled as she tried, unsuccessfully, to get Jodie to engage in a round of patty-cake. If she can endlessly reach for the candle on the window sill, why can't she focus on playing patty-cake?

"Didn't want to startle you," Daphne said as she closed the door behind her and sat across the table.

"No surprises in this warzone!"

"Long day, huh?"

BARRIER ISLANDS

"Wouldn't be so bad if we could get outside." They were into their sixth consecutive day of a cold mist and drizzle as a front had backed in off the ocean and stalled over the island.

"Sometimes the island's shortest days are its longest."

"Tell me about it. I've never liked winter, but this is ridiculous! Get yourself a beer."

Daphne laughed. "The island remedy to all ills! Thanks, but I'll pass."

"On the wagon?"

Daphne shook her head.

"Hungover from last night?"

She laughed. "No. Test tomorrow."

Brooke chuckled, recalling her long ago college days. "Since when did that matter?"

Daphne shrugged and looked away.

"Well, if you're not going to partake, how about getting me one. I've got my hands full at the moment."

Daphne jumped up, got a beer out of the fridge, opened it, and slid it across to Brooke.

Brooke took a long swallow and breathed an audible sigh of relief. Then she noticed Daphne's stare. "If you're counting, this is my first."

Daphne shook her head emphatically. "No. No. I was just thinking you're such a good mother."

Brooke laughed sarcastically. "I was just thinking the exact opposite!" Jodie reached for the beer can.

"Lately, you're never apart from Jodie. It's like she's attached to you."

"Don't I know that, and still she gets into all kinds of mischief!" Jodie kept fighting to touch the can. Brooke finally held it close to her daughter. Jodie wrapped her tiny hands on either side and pulled the can to her lips and nursed on the side of the cold metal.

Daphne laughed. "I wish I had my camera."

"Probably get me arrested."

"Not out here. A rite of passage."

"Babies and beer?"

"Everything and beer."

Brooke took the can back from Jodie. She thought the baby would start crying, but instead she threw herself forward into her mother's chest, in apparent exhaustion or exasperation. The adult gesture startled Brooke.

Daphne laughed. "Already a Howard!"

Brooke laughed too. But something in the remark stuck in her head. She turned the can in her hand, stared at the red and blue print on its white background.

"Are you glad you had Jodie?"

Brooke looked up quickly. "Of course! Why?"

"Just curious. You were so young. Still are!" She laughed then grew serious again. "You had so many other choices."

"I wanted to start my adult life."

"So it wasn't a mistake."

Brooke tried to weigh the meaning of her statement. Though it wasn't voiced as a question, she responded as if it were. "Strictly speaking, the pregnancy wasn't planned. But neither did I take steps to avoid it. I knew the likely outcome."

"And Onion?"

Brooke laughed. "Do boys ever think about that?"

"They should."

"They don't. Never assume they do."

Daphne nodded slowly. "But you did."

"Somewhere beneath all the fireworks? Yes."

"And you're happy the way it turned out?"

Brooke was afraid it would come around to this. She patted the back of Jodie's head, gently brushed her daughter's curly brown hair. Jodie was asleep against her breast. She smiled down then looked up to

Daphne. "How could I not be?" But suddenly tears rose to her eyes. She glanced to the side and quickly blinked them away.

Daphne saw her sister-in-law's reaction as a powerful affirmative answer to her question. After a few seconds, she laughed to break the silence. "That calls for a beer!" She rose and got one out of the fridge and opened it. "To Jodie," she said and raised the can.

"To Jodie," Brooke said and tapped Daphne's can.

They both drank to the sleeping toddler.

"What about your test?" Brooke asked.

"Since when did that matter?" Daphne said.

Brooke laughed then stood to put the subject of their toast to bed.

18

Onion started his Coast Guard training about a month later, in early March. The training divided his time between field work—mostly spent cleaning the small rescue launch or the docked ferries and learning the names of the equipment on board under the supervision of his cousin Frank who everybody called Cracker and was already a First Mate—and classroom study. This consisted of his Uncle Berg or Aunt Dotty pulling a dusty manual off the shelf in Berg's office and dropping it in front of him on the table in the dispatch office. "Memorize this then I'll give you the test," Uncle Berg would say, by which he meant that he would literally give him the test and let him fill in the answers out of the book.

Though the training was not rigorous, it did fill all of Onion's weekdays. Brooke complained that he was "no more than an unpaid government flunky." Onion, when he chose to respond to Brooke's protests, would mutter something about "paying his dues." In any case, Onion was hardly ever home, as he worked nights and weekends at the restaurant to make up for the weekdays spent in training.

And though he stopped smoking pot at home, following Brooke's repeated nagging about "being a bad influence on Jodie," she could tell he was smoking more often out of her sight, both after the restaurant closed (a daily ritual to "take the edge off") and now sometimes while supposedly "in training," probably off with Cracker at the end of the pier or in the break room with the windows open and the fan on. Brooke found it hard to complain about Onion's marijuana use, since it had been a regular feature, and accelerant, to their courtship and early marriage, with her willing participation and occasional encouragement. But since Jodie's birth she rarely smoked and never got high, seeing the activity as a vestige of bygone youth and youthful irresponsibility.

BARRIER ISLANDS 109

So now in the rare moments she saw her husband with both of them awake, he was almost always high. But instead of being the energetic and silly and creative free spirit he used to be when high, he was now mainly silent and sullen, escaping into his own world of non-responsiveness. At times Brooke envied him this escape, which only made her angrier as she realized that escape was now closed to her forever, by choice and circumstance.

As Onion found his escapes—and she could only imagine the full details of those escapes as he sometimes didn't come home at night and other times arrived home disheveled and with the scent of an unfamiliar body clinging to him beneath the smell of pot or alcohol—Brooke explored her own options in this regard. The obvious opportunity was alcohol. With Jodie nursing less, she felt free to imbibe more—sometimes with Daphne but increasingly alone: at first a beer before dinner, then a beer before and with dinner, then a beer before and with and after dinner, sometimes interspersed with shots of rum. It was an easy slope to slide down, took the edge off her day and her loneliness.

Within the haze of that escape, she silently contemplated other escapes. There were lots of men on the island; and almost every one of them—single, divorced, or married—would have been delighted to sample her offerings. Though she'd largely damped her fires of sexual lure since choosing Onion, those fires and their attraction still blazed within her. The obvious choice, and safest, in this possibility was Dave Weldon. She didn't cross paths with his often; but whenever she did, he'd stare calmly, fixing her with those piercing blue eyes. She could've stared right back, matched his taunt, but so far refused to engage in that game. She'd not spoken with let alone touched him since that day in his pick-up, the last day she spoke to Greta. But it was getting more difficult for her to turn away from those stares. And those weren't the only stares that followed her as she ran her errands on the island. Even with Jodie almost always in tow, male eyes both familiar and strange would follow her every sometimes prancing step, the stare often accompanied by a low whistle or suggestive comment. Part of her—indeed, most of her—was glad for these attentions. But she feared what would become of her if she ever accepted those invitations and surrendered to that escape.

Finally there was the escape of a new drug in town, a white powder inhaled through the nose. She'd heard of it in college and had been at a few parties there where others had snorted it. But she'd never tried it until a get-together last fall for a waitress returning to college. The waitress, named Colleen, had pulled out a small vial of the powder and passed the mirror around for all to sample. After the stinging in her nose subsided, Brooke felt an unprecedented sense of euphoria, a formerly impossible combination of energy and comfort, the world both more brilliant and more secure. Colleen recognized the transfixed gaze in Brooke's eyes and jotted a number on a slip of paper "in case you want more than this taste." It was an island number with no name attached to it. Brooke had never dialed that number but kept the slip hidden beneath her underwear drawer.

Opposite these idle and often not so idle—in fact, sometimes quite urgent—musings, stood—or lay or sat or crawled or, just last week, tottered from standing beside the couch into her mother's waiting arms leaning forward from the chair—Jodie. For a brief spell in the dimmest depths of a fog-bound winter, Brooke thought of her daughter as an anchor dragging her down, even backward, into the enslavement of maternity. But with the gradually brightening days reviving youthful needs and hungers within her—she was, after all, still only twenty-two—she began to perceive her daughter as a different kind of anchor, one that kept her from flying off into the realm of self-indulgent escape that had come to define her surroundings. She would picture herself as a bright colored balloon—red, of course—being tugged toward a brilliant blue sky by swirling ocean thermals only to look back and see Jodie seated on the sand in her

BARRIER ISLANDS

sun bonnet firmly clinging to the string that tethered her balloon to earth. This image was planted in her mind one sunny afternoon when Malcolm White sampled his new canister of helium first by inhaling a bit and speaking in a funny squeaky voice and then by inflating a large red balloon and offering it to the mesmerized Jodie who refused to release it all the way through the walk home and her bath and dinner and bedtime story, not even while falling toward sleep. It finally came loose after she fell asleep, as she pulled her hand to her mouth to suck her thumb. Brooke realized that day the tenacity of her daughter's grasp and focus, even so young, and committed herself to match that intensity in her search for a future that would benefit them both, not simply gratify some near-term hungers or needs.

But the path of that search would not be a direct one.

19

Easter morning dawned bright and clear. The overnight chill off the water had been swept away by mid-morning, routed by the brilliant sun and a warm breeze out of the southwest.

The night before, Bridge and Lil had pushed hard for them to attend the sunrise service held on a high dune in the National Seashore. "If God is anywhere," Bridge had claimed, "He'll be in all that water and sky," adding after an appropriate pause and with a touch of awe, "Only place big enough to hold Him." Brooke had frowned but held her silence; Onion, home for once and sober, had gently resisted. "Mighty early, Dad, even for Jodie let alone late-sleeper Brookie!" He'd pinched her under the table and she'd kicked him back but was secretly glad he'd left them an out from the ritual that last year, eight months pregnant and fighting off a cold, was pure torture, standing in the fog singing hymns to a sun that didn't appear that day till after noon.

So when Bridge rapped loudly on their door in the gray pre-dawn and Onion yelled back "You go on ahead. We might meet you later," Brooke breathed an audible sigh of relief and rolled over to return to sleep. But Onion had another plan. His hand eased its way downward over her nightgown and found its way past the hiked up hem and to her panties. "If God is anywhere, he'll be right here," he whispered as he gently ran his finger back and forth on the cotton fabric. She purred in agreement, then reached her hand behind her and found unerring what was waiting at the center of his nakedness (he always slept naked, even in the coldest weather). "Or maybe he's here," she said as she stroked back and forth. He rolled her toward him. "Maybe we should bring your god and my god together." She giggled and said, "Or maybe not." She quickly rose above him and straddled his chest, deftly removed her underwear, then turned around atop him, lifted the covers over her head, and bent over so that her face was at his groin, slid her knees upward till they were at either side of his head. "Keep our gods apart?"

BARRIER ISLANDS

113

he asked. "Safer that way," she said. He briefly wondered what she meant before his mind surrendered to the pleasure of her ministrations and his returning the gift in kind.

Later that morning they slid into the pew beside Bridge and Lil and Daphne just as the organist began playing the opening hymn. The small white clapboard Methodist church was packed. There were only two churches on Shawnituck, Methodist and Baptist; and fortunately for Brooke, who was raised Methodist and had the denomination's requisite disdain for the overly energetic Baptists, the Howards were all Methodists, far back as John Wesley's conversion.

Daphne had all but sprawled across the pew to save their seats against repeated attempts at appropriation. When Brooke finally slid into the pew holding Jodie on her shoulder and followed by Onion, Daphne lifted her eyes and raised her arms as if ready to launch into the Hallelujah chorus. Behind her, Bridge, seated nearest the center aisle, silently shook his head and Lil rolled her eyes above a tight smile of nearly audible relief. Her son and daughter-in-law and granddaughter might have missed the sunrise service; but at least they'd made it to Easter morning worship, and at a moment when everybody in the church couldn't fail to notice.

Just when Brooke had finally settled into the pew and almost caught her breath from the jog while toting Jodie through two backyards and down Gospel Lane, everybody stood for the hymn. She thought she might sit this one out, fussing over Jodie's bonnet as an excuse; but Onion nudged her on the shoulder and gestured with his eyes for her to stand with the rest. She uttered a groan that was inaudible beneath all the singing, slid Jodie off her lap, and slowly stood. Onion offered her half his hymnal, which she took with her right hand while gently patting Jodie's shoulder with her left. By the end of the hymn, her racing heart had slowed, her breaths had calmed, and she felt almost like she belonged there, wedged between her husband and her daughter in this assemblage of islanders.

Everyone was attired in their Easter finest. Brooke and Jodie had on matching lemon-colored dresses with white lace collars that Brooke had sewn over the winter with guidance and advice from Lori Erskine, a Yankee import who now served as the island's seamstress since Belle Argent's arthritis and subsequent dementia. Brooke had also managed to find matching white bonnets with lemon sashes in a catalogue of upscale outfits that Momma had sent her. Though Momma had offered to buy her and Jodie's Easter outfits, Brooke had declined the offer and ordered the bonnets herself. She'd kept the box and all the shipping materials and planned to return the bonnets tomorrow, checking the box marked *wrong size*. But today they fit fine, and Brooke and Jodie were radiant twins between Daphne in her white sleeveless mini-dress and open-toed platform heels and Onion in his black suit, white starched shirt, and burgundy tie. Brooke had found a lemon-colored tie and begged him to wear it for church and the family portrait later this morning, but he had declined with the convenient excuse that he didn't know how to knot a tie and therefore could only use the burgundy one, with its knot preserved from when Miss Polly had tied it before his high school graduation three years ago. Brooke had shrieked in frustration but had no recourse. Though Father could knot a tie in his sleep and she'd often watched him execute the spell-binding sequence during her childhood, she'd never asked to learn the skill.

Jodie was remarkably well-behaved throughout the long service that included two infant baptisms at the small silver font on the white wooden pedestal on wheels that was rolled to the middle aisle prior to the baptisms and rolled away just after. She didn't cry at all and only shrieked once at some hidden delight, a sound that unfortunately came during the prayers and brought muffled giggles from beneath the bowed heads of many of the parishioners. Brooke spent most of the service trying to turn her daughter's attention to the colorful and active surroundings—the church's stained glass side windows, the flickering candles on the altar, the babies being baptized, Aunt Betty Sue's bouncing beehive one pew in front. But all Jodie wanted to do was play with the sash on Brooke's bonnet and poke at the holes in her lace collar. Finally Brooke distracted her by braiding the multi-colored marking ribbons of her hymnal. She'd braid it all the way to the end and tie it off with a knot, then undo the knot and slowly untie the braid, only to begin again when finished. Jodie never tired of watching Brooke's fingers work the bright, thin ribbons in orderly sequence, a rapt attention that recalled Brooke's fascination with her father's knotting his ties.

As they stood for the last hymn, Onion leaned over and whispered, "I'm going to check on the Brunch."

Brooke said, "Don't stain your shirt before the picture!"

"Don't you worry, my Little Brookie." He pinched her waist just above where their thighs touched.

Brooke felt dizzy but quickly recovered.

Onion slid out of the pew. He was headed to the restaurant to check on preparations for the annual Easter Brunch—free and open to all on the island. It was Miss Polly's brainchild dating back since before Onion was born, and his grandmother oversaw the preparations with typical imperious rigor and attention to detail. Earlier in the week when Onion had offered to help, Miss Polly had dismissed the offer with a wave of her hand and a stern command, "Spend the day with that pretty wife of yours and my little Peach Pie." Onion had shrugged in response, to which Polly responded, "I mean it! Pay attention to your family! They are all you've got." Onion reflexively nodded—no one on the island challenged that tone and voice. But now immersed in the commanded task, he couldn't resist slipping away to check on the restaurant that had become his refuge and solace.

JEFFREY ANDERSON

After the service Brooke stood outside the church in the warm sun with Daphne while Lil paraded Jodie around like a trophy for all to see.

"She's in Heaven," Daphne said in a whimsical tone that seemed odd for the day or the setting.

"Granddaughter or grandmother?" Brooke asked.

"I meant Mom. She's made for this. But Jodie seems pretty happy too."

Brooke stared at her sister-in-law, trying to gauge her meaning. Unlike herself, who always spoke without thinking, Daphne rarely made such pronouncements without some deeper reflection. But today she couldn't guess what that reflection might be, and the milling crowd kept her from asking outright. Finally she said, "I suppose."

Daphne looked at her with a big smile. "The two of you looked darling. I can't believe you made the dresses. They're perfect! And the bonnets put us all to shame."

"Thanks. But there's no upstaging you, girlfriend. You're positively radiant!" It was true. Daphne, who had always been a lanky and homely tomboy, seemed to have grown up and found an unassuming natural beauty overnight. The short and simple dress, stylish on the mainland but not out here, might have caught the eye and drawn the most attention; but it was the poised, almost serene, young woman inside it that riveted Brooke's gaze. When had that happened?

"Did you see Tommy drop his program so he could look under the pew?" Tommy was a Howard cousin, Betty Sue and Link's fourteen-year-old surly son.

Brooke nodded. "Par for the course."

"I thought of giving him a peek."

"You didn't?" Brooke said, feigning shock. "Would have made his day."

Daphne laughed. "I kept my legs crossed. He'll have to use his imagination."

"Running wild."

BARRIER ISLANDS

117

Daphne nodded. "But not with my help."

Brooke thought, *He doesn't need any help*, but said nothing. Then she thought suddenly, *Everyone is watching, all the time*, but didn't know what she meant. Were they all watching their private parts, or just watching in general? If the latter, then why? At the moment, no one was watching the two of them standing off to one side in the church's sandy front yard, least far as she could tell.

They waited for Bridge and Lil to finish greeting every single person in the lingering crowd, then walked along the packed sand paths to the restaurant. By the time they got there, it was already jammed with people coming out with brimming plates to find a seat on the front porch or at one of the picnic tables borrowed from the nearby motel and set up in the parking lot. Everybody was in a cheerful mood and said, "Happy Easter!" as they passed. A few said, "He is risen!" but they were all Baptists.

Inside was even more crowded with a line snaking from the buffet table inside the restaurant out into the wide entry foyer.

Miss Polly, seated on her throne that was the stool behind the cash register, spotted them and waved them forward. She grabbed Jodie out of Lil's arms. "Look at my little Peach Pie, dressed up as an Easter princess. Your momma should dress you up more often. You're just cute as a button!" Polly rubbed noses with her great-granddaughter then used her bonnet to play peekaboo.

Bridge and Lil and Daphne and Brooke stood wedged against the register counter smiling indulgently and waiting patiently.

Polly put the bonnet back on Jodie's head and tied the sash under her chin though Jodie didn't like that and tried to untie the knot. "Now you leave that alone," Polly said and pulled Jodie's hands away from the sash. "Let me show you what the Easter Bunny left." She slid off the stool and walked into the dining room through a side door that also led to the kitchen, holding Jodie on her shoulder but paying no heed to the others.

118   JEFFREY ANDERSON

Bridge looked back at the other three, shrugged, then sidled around the end of the counter and followed his mother, with Lil, Daphne, and Brooke trailing behind.

Every table in the restaurant was full except for a long table just outside the two-way swinging doors leading into the kitchen. This was Miss Polly's table and reserved for immediate family. Though it wasn't in any way marked as reserved, everyone on the island knew not to sit at it—unless of course you were Howard kin, and close Howards at that (none of the widely scattered riff-raff). Today at one end of the table was a high chair with a colorful Easter basket sitting in front of it, with lots of sparkling foil-wrapped bunnies and eggs sitting in a nest of green faux grass.

"Look at what the Easter Bunny brought my little Peach Pie!" Polly exclaimed as she carried Jodie to the head of the table. She set her great-granddaughter in the high chair then from under the chair pulled out one of Malcolm's helium balloons, this one a special order of a smiling Easter bunny. Polly then stood back to marvel at her handiwork.

Jodie was in Heaven, overwhelmed with visual and auditory stimuli (the low-ceilinged restaurant was noisy with chatter and laughter and Handel's Messiah playing over the speakers). She looked to the bunny balloon bobbing over her head, to the foil candies in the basket, to the pink pastel paper table cloth and the colorful jellybeans strewn about like marbles, to Polly with her hands clutched under her chin in joyful satisfaction. Jodie looked about with wide-eyed wonder and glee, everywhere except to her mother.

Brooke saw that her baby was well-tended. She thought she should be happy to be relieved of her responsibility if only for a few minutes. She turned toward the buffet table, where the family had immediate backside access, and contemplated all that food. Only then did she realize she was starving, as only Jodie had gotten breakfast before they'd had to rush off to church (and still almost late!). She went and loaded

BARRIER ISLANDS 119

up a plate and found a space only a few seats removed from Miss Polly's glowing Easter princess.

Forty-five minutes later Brooke sat in that same chair in the slightly dazed fog of that huge breakfast atop all the morning's activities. She was now alone at the table as Miss Polly was out front greeting departing guests and Bridge and Lil were once again parading Jodie around the slowly thinning crowd of diners and Daphne had disappeared without eating and the rest of the Howard clan that had so recently packed their table had all dispersed. And who knows where Onion was? He'd stopped by the table halfway through her meal, shed of his suitcoat and with the lower half of his tie tucked into his shirt between two buttons. He'd given her a hug and pinched Jodie's nose before rushing back into the kitchen. At least his shirt was still unstained.

Brooke felt a sudden wave of nausea, promptly stirring her from her daze. She covered her mouth to hold in what might soon be coming out and rushed to the restaurant's only public bathroom. Jock Barr was just emerging from that restroom and gave her a big smile before seeing her urgency and jumping aside. She slammed the door behind, dropped to her knees on the slimy floor (raising her dress hem before she did), then dropped her hand from her mouth and regurgitated the entire mass of eggs, sausage, biscuits, gravy, and coffee into the toilet's bowl. She closed her eyes against the gross sight but couldn't ward off the awful stink of vomit mixed with urine and poop smells. This combination of odors produced another spasm in her gut, then another. This third was dry but worse than the first two for the wrenching in her gut that radiated into her throat. She lay her head on her arm on the toilet seat in exhaustion.

She reached up with her free hand and pulled the lever. The bowl roared as its contents swirled then slowly emptied and refilled with clean water flecked with a few floating pieces of egg and biscuit. She pulled the lever again. The unique odor combined with the sound of flushing recalled a memory from one morning her first week working at the restaurant two summers ago. Miss Polly had handed her a mop and pointed at the bathroom and said, "Go clean up Mary's mess." One of their customers, a free-spirited and single islander named Mary Pickett, had lost her breakfast in this very bathroom. But she had missed the bowl; and newcomer Brooke, low girl in the pecking order, was left with the task of cleaning it up. Halfway through the unpleasant chore, Onion, whom she'd only just met, came up behind with a bucket of Lysol and helped out, bending low and getting the pieces she'd missed under the bowl and behind the tank. As they'd finished, he'd given her the air freshener to spray then picked up the bucket of dirty liquid to dump outside the kitchen. He'd bent close to her ear and whispered, "Guess Mary's knocked up. Wonder who the father is?" He'd grinned that silly grin she'd grow to adore, winked, then headed off with the bucket.

At the time she didn't get the connection. Six months later, Mary gave birth to a baby boy. By then, Brooke herself was three months pregnant and understood all too well the connection Onion had spotted. There's only one reason otherwise healthy young women lose their breakfast.

When Brooke emerged from the bathroom, after checking her dress and washing her hands and rinsing her mouth and splashing a little cold water on her face, she was relieved to see no one waiting. And apparently none had noted her absence. The dining room was empty. Everyone was in the entry or outside. Only Jock had witnessed the incident and he didn't gossip. She again checked her dress and shoes, grabbed a jellybean off the table to cover the foul taste in her mouth, then headed outside to join the others.

In the family photo taken in front of the restaurant fifteen minutes later, Onion's shirt is unstained, burgundy tie trimly knotted, suitcoat buttoned; Jodie's brown curls cascade out from under her bonnet, its sash primly but loosely tied under her chin; and Brooke has a stiff smile pasted on her face, her bonnet missing, her skin a little pale despite the bright day.

20

Though in her heart Brooke knew what was going on—her missed period, her sensitive breasts and sexual appetite gone into the stratosphere, and now this incident at the Brunch—she felt she needed medical proof. She could go to her obstetrician or the Howard family doctor, both on the mainland; but appointments with either would rouse suspicions and raise too many questions, and Brooke was a terrible liar. Home pregnancy tests had recently become available, but the general store didn't yet carry them. Even if it did, purchase of such a kit would've been island news even before the change had settled in her pocket.

She considered soliciting Daphne's advice and help. Her sister-in-law had produced stellar and totally secret results with the condom request, despite the ultimate failure—in usage, not availability—of the gift. But she decided not to put Daphne in the middle of this development and whatever decisions might arise from it. Daphne was, in the end, a Howard.

And Brooke was a Fulcher. Easter night, with Jodie to bed early after her full day and Onion off supposedly cleaning up the restaurant (closed for the holiday after the Brunch) but who knows what that meant, Brooke sat at the kitchen table and jotted off a note on a lined pad:

Dear Leah,

Please send a pregnancy test in an unmarked box. And hurry! I'll explain later.

Brooke

Brooke folded the note and slid it into an envelope. But before sealing the flap, she paused and thought about how she'd failed to

BARRIER ISLANDS

123

respond to her sister's three letters since Christmas—two before Greta's death (mainly news about classes and college life) and one shortly after the funeral (unburdening Leah's grief at the loss and trying to get Brooke to open up about hers). She pulled the note out of the envelope, unfolded it, and added the following:

P. S. Sorry I haven't written. Life has been crazy. I miss you. B.

By then tears flooded her eyes, but she made sure none dropped on the paper. She refolded the note and slid it back in the envelope, then sealed, addressed, and stamped it. She'd post it early the next day to go out on the noon "mailboat" which now consisted of a locked canvas sack delivered to the mainland via the ferry but was still called the mailboat in reference to—some might say reverence for—the bygone supply boat that had served the island, in various incarnations, for centuries until it was replaced a few years back by regular state-run ferry service.

21

Later that week, on a chilly and fog-bound day that seemed a return to winter and when Onion had gone straight from Coast Guard training to the restaurant and before she had got a response from her letter to Leah, Brooke was carrying Jodie from the couch where she'd changed her diaper and put on her pajamas to the crib to put her to bed when she hooked her foot on the leg of the coffee table and lost her balance. As she started to fall, she instinctively did two things. She tightened her arms around her daughter and she rotated herself so that her body would hit the wood floor first and Jodie would land on top of her, not vice versa. But with this combination of maneuvers, she fell toward the couch. The side of her face hit the wooden arm of the couch, then the back of her head smacked the floor.

When she returned to consciousness, Jodie was lying on top of her chest, sniffling and gasping like she did after crying hard for several minutes. "It's O.K., baby girl," Brooke whispered. She wiped the tears from Jodie's eyes and brushed her hair and ran her fingers over her daughter's head. There were no bumps or blood that she could see. Jodie's crying and gasping gradually calmed. Brooke used her arms to raise Jodie first to a sitting position then a standing one atop her chest. Jodie's appendages were all in their former placement and in working order. Brooke began to cry then. She pulled Jodie down and hugged her to her chest. "I'm so sorry, baby girl."

Jodie quit sniffling and said, "Mommy."

Though Jodie had been making intentional sounds for weeks and those sounds recently started to be directed toward particular objects or people, this was her first clear use of a word for her mother. Brooke stopped crying and raised her daughter far enough above her chest to see her face. "Yes, baby girl. I am your mommy."

Jodie didn't repeat the word, but her lips turned upward in a smile.

BARRIER ISLANDS 125

Brooke slowly sat up, keeping Jodie in her lap. With one hand supporting Jodie, she used the other to check the stinging left side of her face, near her eye socket, then the back of her head. Lumps were rising in both spots, but there was no blood or open wounds. She felt dizzy and leaned against the side of the couch. Jodie leaned forward against her chest, and Brooke draped both arms around her daughter. They both closed their eyes.

After some time passed, Brooke opened her eyes, laid Jodie on the couch, then slowly stood by rolling onto her hands and knees and using the couch for support as she rose. Her whole body ached. But her legs and feet, arms and hands all functioned normally. She took several deep breaths to help clear her head, then picked up the sleeping Jodie and gently laid her in the crib before preparing two ice packs for the throbbing bumps on her head.

The next morning, shortly before heading off to training, Onion lifted his glazed eyes and looked at his wife sitting across the table feeding Jodie her breakfast. He blinked several times and shook himself awake. "What the hell happened to you?" he asked when he realized the purple bruise on the side of her face and spreading to the soft tissue under her eye wasn't a shadow or a sleep mark.

"I tripped."

Onion waited a few seconds then said, "And?"

"And I hit the side of the couch. I'll be O.K."

Onion reached across the table and used his fingers to turn Brooke's face into the light.

Brooke tolerated the examination briefly before jerking her face away and returning to feeding Jodie.

"I was just checking you, Brooke! Trauma evaluation is part of our training."

"Go train on somebody else. I'm fine!"

Onion stood and left, headed out into the pre-dawn dark to open up the Coast Guard office and continue his training.

Everyone who saw Brooke's black eye assumed Onion had hit her. Nobody said so in words, but Brooke could tell it by the way they acted. Men would squint or flinch and look away. Women would gaze in sympathy, with some lightly touching her hand. She didn't make any effort to correct them. Domestic abuse, particularly in late winter and early spring, was so ubiquitous on the island that trying to offer an alternative explanation, however truthful, was hopeless. "Of course you tripped and fell, darling. We've all done that." She let it go and hoped the bruise would disappear soon.

Of much greater concern was her shaken confidence in her ability to fulfill her maternal responsibilities. She could not convince herself that the fall was simply an accident and not the result of the four beers she'd drunk in fairly rapid succession while also skipping dinner. She'd never questioned her ability to love and care for her baby. It would always be her first and foremost calling. But in those lonely days following her fall, when she would frequently look at her face in the mirror and see the ever darkening bruise staring back, she wasn't sure she could trust herself in that primary duty.

Further complicating this inner struggle was the spotting that appeared in her panties the morning after the fall. That spotting turned into fairly heavy bleeding accompanied by some atypical cramping over the following days. After hardly being sick a day in her life, her entire body seemed to be rebelling, ached everywhere. Worse, her physical pain and emotional confusion came complete with outer symbols—blood, and not blood that was bright and red with life but blood that was dark and stale, purple to black.

BARRIER ISLANDS

A box arrived from Leah on the Monday mailboat. At first Brooke didn't open it, then she did. It contained not one but two pregnancy test kits and a neatly folded note on expensive pale-green stationery with Leah's initials embossed in gold at the top.

Dear Brooke,
Do you need me there? Let me know and I'll be on the next
ferry.
Love,
Leah

Brooke hid the pregnancy kits in the back of her t-shirt drawer, along with Leah's note. She jotted a quick response:

Thanks, Sis. I'm O.K.
Now go study. Better yet, ask one of those charming hunks out
to dinner.
I love you.
Brooke.

22

Three weeks into spring—though it hardly felt it, gray and damp and cold as it was with a raw wind off the ocean—Brooke was warming some turkey soup for her dinner after feeding Jodie when she heard a shrill scream that came from Bridge and Lil's house. She paused. The scream was followed by a long low moan like the sound of a large animal dying.

Her first reaction was to run next door. But before taking a step in that direction, she stopped to assess her priorities. She needed to turn off the burner under the soup pot. She needed to get Jodie out of the high chair and either put her in her crib or carry her with her. While she weighed that choice, she used a damp cloth to clean the applesauce from around Jodie's mouth then removed her bib. She lifted Jodie out of the chair and carried her to the crib and set her down in it. Jodie stood holding the rail and looking at her mother.

"I've got to go check on Mee-mee," Brooke said while squatting to Jodie's height. Jodie had just recently, and spontaneously, started calling Lil "Mee-mee." "I'll be right back." She turned to rush out the door.

"Mommy!" Jodie cried.

Brooke froze then turned back to her daughter. She leaned over and hugged her, considered again taking Jodie but was afraid what she might find. She didn't want to scar her daughter for life with some horrific sight. Another long low scream came from next door. "I love you, darling. Be a good girl. I'll be right back."

She turned again and this time ignored her daughter's cries and went out the door and across the breezeway and opened the side door to her in-laws' house.

Dinner was on the kitchen table with three places set but no one there. "Bridge? Lil?" Brooke said in a cautious and timid voice. She stood for a moment to test the sounds in the house. Another moaning cry punctured the stillness. It clearly came from upstairs. Brooke ran

BARRIER ISLANDS 129

down the hall and up the narrow stairs. When she reached the upper landing, she saw a light on in Daphne's room. Her heart fell into her stomach. She knew she was running but felt as if her body was in slow motion. Her heart raced. Her breaths came shallow and fast. She felt dizzy but pushed onward.

She paused in the open doorway to Daphne's room and grabbed onto the door jamb to steady herself and catch her breath. Lil was lying face down on Daphne's twin bed, crying into the mattress. Bridge sat beside her, patting her back. But where was Daphne? What had happened to Daphne?

"Bridge?" Brooke said.

Bridge turned his head slowly. He looked at Brooke but didn't seem to recognize her. His eyes looked dazed, far away.

"Bridge, it's Brooke. What has happened? Where's Daphne?"

Bridge shook his head slowly. Lil shrieked into the mattress.

"Where is Daphne?" Brooke repeated.

"I'll kill him," Bridge said slowly and in a low growl. His far away gaze hardened into quiet fury.

"Who? What?" Brooke asked, though she instinctively exhaled in a long sigh.

Bridge reached out with his free hand and took a piece of notebook paper off the nightstand. He held it toward Brooke in a gesture caught between surrender and outrage, his pudgy hand and thick forearm shaking.

Brooke discovered that her legs were strong again and stepped forward the two strides to take the white paper. Written on it in Daphne's tall, open script was this message: *I've left with Ralph. Please don't try to find us. I'll write soon. I promise. I love you. Daphne.*

Brooke's sigh became audible. Daphne was safe. She'd run away with Ralph Hopson, the school's art teacher that had so freely shared his personal darkroom with his promising student. Daphne was safe.

But why hadn't Brooke seen this coming? Daphne rarely spoke about her teacher; and when she did, she almost always called him Mr. Hopson. Brooke had never seen the two of them together. She realized suddenly that this was all planned on Daphne's part, to keep their relationship secret. So why hadn't Daphne confided in Brooke? She felt they were close, then reminded herself of how much in her personal life she'd kept from Daphne. She'd always thought of her choice as protecting her sister-in-law, not forcing her to choose sides. But she suddenly knew that she was also protecting herself with these secrets, ensuring that they not be accidentally or intentionally divulged. In her head she trusted Daphne; but in her gut, she still knew Daphne to be a Howard.

Lil screamed again. "My baby!" she wailed into the mattress, the words ending in another moan.

Brooke circled around the bed, set the note on the dresser, then sat next to Lil and opposite Bridge. She patted Lil's flecked gray hair and said, "Daphne's safe. She'll be all right. She's safe."

"She's gone!" Lil screamed. "She'll never come back."

Brooke shook Lil's shoulder. "Lil, look at me."

Her mother-in-law rolled her head enough to look up with one tear-swollen eye.

"Can you help me, please?"

Lil didn't answer but at least she had stopped crying.

"Can you take care of Jodie for a little while?"

Lil rolled onto her side.

"If you'll watch Jodie, I'll go and try to find out a little more about this."

Lil nodded slowly.

"Good. You and Bridge go back downstairs and eat your dinner. I'll go get Jodie."

Lil hesitated.

"Please?" Brooke said. "I need you to watch Jodie for me."

BARRIER ISLANDS

131

Lil sat up.

Brooke circled back around the bed and stood before the two of them. "Don't raise a stink till I've checked this out, O.K.? We don't need the whole island gossiping about your daughter."

Lil nodded. Bridge stared hard at Brooke.

"O.K., Bridge?"

He nodded slowly.

Brooke said, "Good. I'll put Jodie in her PJs and be right back."

She turned. Only then did she notice all of Daphne's photos covering the walls. Then she remembered Daphne's questions about whether or not she was glad she'd had Jodie. And suddenly it hit her—Daphne was pregnant with Ralph Hopson's child.

When Brooke returned with Jodie, Lil had just finished warming their dinner and setting it on the table in serving bowls—country-style steak smothered in fried onions and peppers, mashed potatoes, butterbeans with fatback, and Lil's special yeast rolls. Daphne's place setting had been cleared and her chair replaced by the wooden highchair from their children's infancy that Bridge had sanded and refinished for Jodie's use.

Lil's eyes were dry and surprisingly bright as she ran forward to take Jodie. "How's my darling this evening?" she said with an edge of desperation to her voice—or perhaps that was Brooke's imagination. "Have you come to join Mee-mee and Paw-paw for dinner?" Though Jodie had yet to name her grandfather, Lil was strongly pushing her suggestion.

Bridge sat unblinking at his seat at the head of the table.

Jodie looked at her grandmother with wide eyes. Though she often ate lunch here and sometimes Sunday dinner, this visit for supper was unprecedented.

132 JEFFREY ANDERSON

Brooke kissed her daughter on the side of the forehead. "I'm going out for a little, baby. Mee-mee will take care of you till I get back." She handed Jodie to Lil. She wanted to offer further reassurance about Daphne but feared mentioning the name. So she said simply, "I'll be back by nine," and headed out the door.

A front had moved in with a stiff wind out of the north clearing away the fog. The stars sparkled in number and clarity that still dazzled this former city girl, now nearly two years into her stay out here. She paused in the middle of the empty lane and wondered if by chance Daphne was looking at these same stars at this same moment. Then she realized that more than likely she was in some motel bed stretched out under Ralph doing what apparently they did best and without protection! Brooke sighed with a wonder tinged with envy, recalling the blind hope and trust unimpeded touch had produced in her life not so long ago.

She walked to the ferry station through the brisk dark. Buck Custis was still manning the dispatch office, monitoring the Queen Anne's final crossing of the day via the shortwave radio.

"Hey, Brooke. What brings you out?"

"Getting a little air, Buck. How's the crossing going?"

"Same old, same old. Little chop with the front, head wind pushing her back about five minutes. Expecting someone?"

Brooke paused. "See Daphne today?"

Buck nodded. "Pedestrian on the noon boat. Heard her tell Marybelle she had a doctor's appointment. Found it odd she was walking, but that ain't my business."

Brooke nodded slowly.

"Thought I'd see her coming back on the six o'clock, but no walkers on that one. Figured maybe I missed her in one of the cars—Sally's or maybe Salt's. They came through at six."

"Yeah. Could be."

"What's wrong, Brooke?"

BARRIER ISLANDS   133

"Nothing. Nothing wrong. Just trying to catch up with Daphne."

"Then why don't you check with Lil?"

"Sure. I'll do that. Just thought I'd save myself the trip."

"Next door?"

Brooke laughed. "You know how it gets with in-laws sometimes."

"No, I don't. Never had none."

Buck was a life-long bachelor. Brooke sometimes wondered if he were gay. If so, she guessed he had lean pickings out here—but then again, what did she know about this island's secrets? "Little tricky sometimes. No big deal."

Buck shrugged. "So I've heard."

"Enjoy the pretty night," Brooke said. She turned to head out the door.

Behind her, Buck said, "You too. Hope you find Daffy."

"Thanks." Then, just before the door closed, she caught it with her foot and turned. "You haven't seen Ralph Hopson around, have you?"

"The school teacher?"

"Yeah, the young one with the curly hair."

"And blue eyes." Buck suddenly blushed.

"Yeah, blue eyes and dimples," Brooke laughed. "He owes me five bucks for the church peanut sale."

"That was back before Christmas."

"I know! That's why I'm trying to collect."

"Well good luck. He was on the ten o'clock and his van was loaded down—had the curtains drawn across the back but I could see the weight on the tires. I told Jess to put him near the middle of the boat."

"Maybe he was headed back to college for his finals," Brooke suggested.

"No. I believe he'd graduated. Paying off his loans by working out here."

"Oh, yeah," Brooke said.

"Then why's he leaving before school is out?"

Brooke shrugged. "Maybe a family emergency."

"With all his stuff?"

"Good night, Buck." She turned toward the dark.

"Good luck."

She faced back. "With what?"

"Getting your five dollars!" He laughed.

"Oh, yeah. Right." She waved and headed into the night.

As she was passing the gate to the dock, a foghorn blast rolled in off the water, its sound strangely mournful despite the clear, brisk night. The lights of the Queen Anne twinkled far out on the horizon, between the pervasive dark of the water and the sparkling dome of the night. She could wait a half hour and talk to the crew, but what was the point? She knew the means of their escape. She now had to find out, or confirm, why. She headed back into the village.

Though only a ten-minute walk over a familiar road, it was the loneliest ten minutes Brooke had ever spent in her life. The island was so dark and still and somehow foreboding. Though she could have walked this path with her eyes closed (and maybe should have), it felt suddenly strange and hostile. She'd not been on this end of the island after dark since before she was married, and back then always accompanied by another—always a man and, after a handful of fun but unpromising frolics, always with Onion and safely wrapped in the promise of his touch and scent. Tonight was brutally empty. She hastened her step and was glad for the shelter and shadow of buildings on the outskirts of the village, even though the first structures were all empty cottages and businesses closed till summer.

She stopped at The Shipwreck, the only tavern open in the off-season. She was looking for Deena Windlass, Daphne's best friend who had graduated from the island's school the year before despite dropping out two years earlier to work in her dad's tavern. She laughed at the diploma, saying it was for "the best kind of work study—people watching and beer drinking."

BARRIER ISLANDS

Deena was sitting at the bar beside Jim Walker, universally known as Snaggletooth, who spent most of his time and slim earnings here despite having three kids and a wife sequestered in a camper hidden in the marshes on the sound side. Brooke paused in the doorway to let her eyes adjust to the indoor light but then realized she didn't have to as the bar was nearly as dark as the lane outside.

"Well look who's here—the savior of the Howard line," Deena said with a gravelly voice and a low laugh. "Come join the party!"

Brooke approached the bar. "Got a minute to talk?"

"Let me see if I have time in my busy schedule." She paused and looked around then said, "Yeah, I guess I can spare a minute. Better talk fast!"

"In private?" Brooke asked, gesturing toward a table at the far end of the narrow room.

"You can talk here. Snaggletooth don't hear nothing, do you Snaggletooth?"

"Huh?" Snaggletooth said.

"See?"

Brooke said, "Please, Deena. It's important."

"Oh, all right," Deena said. She grabbed her cigarette and her beer bottle and slid off the barstool. "Now don't go and steal nothing," she said to Snaggletooth.

"Huh?"

Deena laughed and followed Brooke to the far table. Before sitting, she asked, "You want anything?"

Brooke shook her head.

"Got juice, or a Shirley Temple. Heard you were off the sauce at the moment."

"Where did you hear that?"

Deena shrugged. "Around."

"No thanks. I'm fine."

Deena sat opposite Brooke at the table. She stared at her as she took a drag on the cigarette. "You're here about Daffy," she said before releasing a long thin line of smoke out of the corner of her mouth.

"How'd you know?"

"Howard daughter flees the island with her teacher! How could I not know news big as that?"

Brooke held her finger to her lips then looked over Deena's shoulder at Jim.

"Oh, stop, Brooke. Snaggletooth don't know nothing and won't know it from me. He's got way bigger problems than this." Still, she lowered her voice. "Besides, everyone on the island will know tomorrow morning."

"Know what exactly?"

"What you already figured out—that Daffy Howard and Ralph Hopson are long gone and ain't coming back, headed to South Carolina to get hitched."

Brooke winced in surprise.

"Hadn't figured that part out? What you think they were going to do? Live in sin? Raise a bastard? Daffy would never do that."

Brooke exhaled slowly.

Deena continued. "And even if she were willing, noble idealist teacher-boy would have none of it. 'Need to make this right' he said as he banged his student every way he knew how. That's what kills me about these mainlanders that are going to save us from ourselves. Their ideals last only to the end of their dicks then get thrown overboard like a wriggling mess of bycatch. Maybe I should let a mainlander save me one day, or night." She took a long swallow of beer then belched. "Then again, maybe I have—a time or two." She grinned at the thought. "But I'd never leave with him."

"Why not?"

"I couldn't live that lie."

"And Daphne?"

BARRIER ISLANDS

Deena thought for a moment then said, "I hope she knows what she's doing. She sure thinks she does."

"Not coming back?"

"Not in this lifetime." Deena raised the cigarette and took a long drag. Her thin and weathered face looked suddenly very old and gray, grayer even than the room's dim light.

Brooke wandered through the quiet empty village. There were a few lights on in some of the buildings, and every so often she'd catch a glimpse of movement behind a window—a body shuffling from kitchen to couch, a cat jumping from a windowsill, the flash of activity on a black and white T.V. screen. She no longer felt threatened by the emptiness, but she did feel unspeakably lonely. Deena's last words bounced around in her head like an epitaph.

She stepped into the general store's vestibule to escape the night. It was well lit and close and still warm form the daytime traffic in and out of the store. Though the store had closed at six, the vestibule allowed access to the village's mailboxes. She'd not checked theirs since yesterday morning and did so now. Between two catalogues and the electric bill was an envelope with her name on it but no address or stamp. She recognized the handwriting as Daphne's. Daphne had a part-time job (or did) at the store and had access to the mailboxes. She must have left this late yesterday or possibly even this morning on her way to the ferry. Brooke tore open the envelope and read the handwritten letter while leaning against the mailboxes.

Dear Brooke,

I'm sorry I didn't say good-bye in person. I knew I couldn't do so without crying, and I've already cried way too much this week. Do you know how hard it is to cry in private then have to put on a smile for all

138 JEFFREY ANDERSON

those around you? Yes, you probably do know that. I'm sure you do. One more thing we have in common.

I wish to thank you for opening my eyes to the possibilities of life. I knew I wasn't meant for this island, but it wasn't until you came that I saw an alternative. You showed me that a woman could be her own person, with goals and dreams, and not just the appendage of a husband or father, or some old maid dusting her tea set waiting for company that never comes. A girl could have an identity independent of a family. You opened my eyes to that then Ralph opened my eyes to everything else, to art and music and poetry and photography. And suddenly I was flying. You know about that too.

I still haven't heard back from Center. The decision notices go out next month. I would have liked to open that letter with you beside me, to cry or shriek in joy. I never would have dreamed of getting in there or even applying. But with your support and connections, I now halfway think I'll be accepted. It would have been so much fun to share that with you!

But then I might've been tempted to go. Besides, by then I'd be showing and Dad would kill Ralph and my baby wouldn't have a father. So instead I'll keep the baby and her father (I know it's a she, just like Jodie!) and go to college later, maybe to Center or maybe somewhere else but I will go, I promise. And even though I'm not going now, know that all the support and encouragement you gave me, about applying to Center and everything else, was still worth it, gave me the strength to be a whole person, my own person.

Give Jodie a hug for me. One of the biggest regrets I have is not being there to watch her grow up. If I send you an address, will you send me pictures?

There I go crying again. You'd think I'd run out of tears.

Take care, Brooke. Thanks for bringing me to life.

Your crying and flying sister-in-law,

Daphne

23

"You caused this!" Onion screamed the next morning.

"Caused what?"

"You know damn well what I'm talking about!"

"If you mean Daphne running away, I had no idea. I was just as shocked as everyone else."

"Filling her head with crazy ideas. Telling her she should go to college and helping her fill out the application!"

"She's a bright girl, Onion. What was she supposed to do—stay here and stock shelves the rest of her life? Wait tables?"

"Tend her family—same as her momma and grandma."

"Same as me and Jodie?"

Onion almost said something but swallowed his words. "You put her up to this. You might as well have packed her bags and bought her crossing ticket."

"I gave her choices. If she'd wanted to take a job here and settle with a local guy, I'd have been behind her all the way. But she's smart, Onion. She needed to stretch her wings. All I did was support what she was already saying and doing. That's what friends are supposed to do. That's what family is supposed to do."

"And look what came of it!"

"Maybe if you'd given her a little more space to grow, she wouldn't have needed to act so—." Brooke paused before adding, "Dramatically."

"Is that what you call screwing your teacher and running off with him?"

"If you'd given her more space, she might have gone to college, got her degree, met a guy, and brought him back here to raise a family. A little outside blood would be good for your family and the island."

"Like you? We see how well that's turned out."

"What's that supposed to mean?"

"You showed up and now Daffy's gone. You figure it out. You're a smart girl." He turned and left.

24

Two weeks later was Jodie's first birthday. Though her actual birthday was on a Sunday, Miss Polly closed the restaurant after lunch that Saturday and had the Howard clan and a few (about two dozen) privileged friends over for a party. They put out pink and white streamers that morning after breakfast then unleashed a hundred pink and white helium-filled balloons (Malc had to order a second canister of helium) after the lunch crowd had exited. With all that pink and white and spring sun streaming through the windows, the dining room looked as cheerful and bright as ever, and all for Jodie. Outside on the porch was almost as festive, with more streamers and clustered balloons tied to the railing posts and a *Happy Birthday* banner over the steps and Bridge's gift of a home-made and hand-painted rocking horse covered with ribbons and bows in the middle of the floor. Miss Polly had floated the idea of Salt bringing a pony over on the ferry, but Brooke (through Onion) had nixed that plan, saying that Jodie was way too young for a pony ride and terrified of any animal larger than a medium-sized dog.

Jodie herself was gaily attired in a new pink jumpsuit and matching sun hat, all hand-sewed by Lil, and white knit booties from Miss Polly. She looked cute as could be with her brown curls flowing from under the hat and her round face all smiles and giggles, her dark eyes dancing. Perhaps somehow knowing this was a special occasion and she was the center of attention, Jodie was animated and alert, talking up a storm (though still mainly gibberish) and pointing to all the newly added decorations as well as some of the old familiar favorites—a hand-carved bluefish, a stuffed deer head—hanging on the walls.

Though Brooke had always freely shared Jodie at these celebrations, today she insisted on keeping her close, holding her on her hip or shoulder as they made their way through the greeting crowd gathered on the porch and bouncing her on her knees as they sat beside the center table with its four-layered cake and the presents laid out all around it. This new and unprecedented possessiveness startled and annoyed the numerous guests who approached with outstretched arms. Brooke deflected these requests with the claim that Jodie was recovering from being sick. She'd had a runny nose last week; but that had been a chronic condition through the damp winter, used as a convenient excuse now. Brooke didn't know why she was suddenly so protective, though it was surely more for her sake than her daughter's, as Jodie responded to those outstretched and welcoming arms with a reciprocal gesture, adding to the guests' frustration. On being denied holding privileges, Miss Polly got so mad she stormed off into the kitchen and didn't return for twenty minutes. Onion glared at Brooke before chasing after his grandmother.

Though she didn't give up Jodie, Brooke did politely greet each of the guests as they streamed by. She'd not had such an opportunity to speak with her extended family of in-laws and their inner circle of island acquaintances since the wedding a year and a half ago, and on that day she was far too caught up in the rush and wonder of events to pay attention to the faces that streamed past in the receiving line. Back then they seemed almost ethereal in their quiet and unassuming presence, fellow occupants in this new Eden. Today those same people were all too human with sea-weathered faces, bloodshot eyes, and lop-sided grins shaped around cooing baby talk. They all focused on Jodie with a desperation that surprised and frightened Brooke. She understood why they didn't look directly at her. She was still, perhaps permanently, marked by Greta's death and now Daphne's departure. Brooke the mainland bride had become Brooke the tainted interloper. Maybe such a transformation was inevitable, and maybe she was at fault; but for the life of her, Brooke couldn't understand why. She clung tightly to Jodie, smiled up at each guest even if they wouldn't meet her eyes, and thanked them for coming and for the gifts that would be opened later.

Late in the party, after the singing of "Happy Birthday" and the blowing out of the candles (Jodie watched in wonder as Brooke and Onion blew out the dozens of small candles surrounding the tall candle in the shape of the number "1") and the sharing of slices of cake with vanilla ice cream scooped from the big tub, Brooke felt the familiar trickle of wetness between her legs. She instinctively checked the color of her pants—jeans in a dark blue denim, probably safe—before looking around for someone to hand Jodie to.

Miss Polly had returned from the kitchen for the singing and cake cutting and was standing at the head of the serving table overseeing the final stages of the party, confirming that there were still enough napkins and forks and that the used plates were being cleared (by Joanne, a new waitress hired to cover this private party) and that the ice cream sitting in the ice filled cooler wasn't melting too fast. She would have loved to claim Jodie and hold her aloft as the day's prize, and deserved as much for all the preparations and effort. But when she looked toward Brooke with censure, Brooke quickly looked away.

She saw Lil sitting off in a corner, not talking to anyone and gazing out the window at the restaurant's back yard with the row of trashcans partially hid by the big black cast-iron pig cooker. She'd not been doing well since Daphne's departure and the sudden and unexpected dose of empty nest blues that came with it. Few on the island had ever experienced such a condition, and Lil never thought she'd have to. But here it was, ready or not.

Brooke stood, glanced quickly at her jeans and was relieved to see no mark there—yet. She walked over to her mother-in-law and asked, "Would you hold Jodie while I visit the little ladies' room?"

Lil glanced up in surprise then smiled broadly as Jodie extended her arms toward her. "Mee-mee."

Lil laughed. "At your service, Precious."

144   JEFFREY ANDERSON

Brooke knew the service and the endearment were directed toward her daughter and was fine with that, felt a sudden swell of munificence. "Take care of your Mee-mee for me," she said to Jodie as she passed her into the arms of Lil. She then scurried to the bathroom.

The nearer public toilet, the one where she'd had the incident on Easter, was occupied. So she pushed through the swinging doors and passed through the empty kitchen to the employee restroom at the back. She pulled the door shut and dropped the hook into the eye to lock it and switched on the light and the fan. She pulled down her jeans and her panties and saw in the crotch the familiar smear of brown-tinged red. This was her first period since the bleeding after her fall and confirmed what her body had been telling her—that she'd miscarried the early-term fetus, and that her body was returning to its former monthly cycling. Her first response was relief—that her body was O.K., not irreparably scarred. But this relief quickly gave way to a mix of intense and contradictory emotions. Part of her was deeply saddened not to be pregnant. She loved being a mother and wanted more kids. But not now, not here. This prompted a deeper relief—that she'd not have to make the impossible choice to terminate her pregnancy. Finally, the face that stared back at her from the small square mirror was tinged with an unfamiliar guilt—that she'd so thoroughly mismanaged her life as to instigate a sequence of calamitous events: multiple reckless couplings, an unplanned pregnancy, and the drunken fall that ended it.

She turned from that guilt-ridden visage. She had no purse and therefore no tampon or pad available. She considered carefully folding multiple layers of toilet paper and placing that wad in her panties, a bulky and uncomfortable temporary solution she'd not used since high school. Then she remembered a secret and reached up under the wall-hung sink. Sure enough, there it was—a plastic holder wedged behind the plumbing that held two tampons. Daphne had showed it to her that first summer out here, one night when they were working together. "Just in case," she'd said. At the time, Brooke had wondered that this skinny flat-chested girl had ever had a period, but thanked her for the tip. She'd not used it back then, being on the pill at the time and regular and meticulously prepared. But here it was now, a late gift from a faraway sister-in-law. Then Brooke realized that Daphne herself hadn't needed tampons recently, all the while without Brooke knowing. The wry grin that stared back from the mirror was both poignant and forlorn.

25

The next morning Brooke was again holding Jodie on her hip. These days it seemed all she was doing, or wanted to do, during waking hours. In familiar spaces, Jodie had grown impatient with being held, wanted to get down so she could try out her newfound walking skills or drop to her hands and knees to race around and explore. She was becoming so willful and insistent! *I wonder where she got that from?* Brooke thought to herself.

But this morning Jodie was happy for the comfort and reassurance of being in her mother's grasp. They were at the stern railing of the ferry as it cleared the harbor breakwater and began its resolute thrust toward the mainland. Brooke had insisted on visiting her family as part of Jodie's birthday celebrations—"She's a year old, Onion; and my family has seen her all of once!" And Onion had reluctantly consented, though he refused to join them. "Can't miss that much training," he'd said.

They were traveling on the near-empty Sunday morning crossing—just three cars of early departure weekenders headed to who knows what lives inland, and all of them holed up tight in their vehicles eating cereal-bar and canned-soda breakfasts or catching a few extra minutes of sleep. So mother and daughter had the aft deck to themselves.

Brooke gazed at the receding village. The spring sun washed those worn buildings in a freshening light. Surrounded by sparkling blue water, it seemed a quaint and self-contained scene from a highly detailed diorama or one of those intricately crafted Christmas snow globes, as if she could give the whole world a good, firm shake, watch all those tiny white specks swirl and blur the vision, only to have the particles slowly drift earthward, again revealing the quaint and rustic island village in morning sun. Whatever she had once seen in that village, *felt* in it, was now gone, lost forever in that swirl.

BARRIER ISLANDS

Brooke knew she was leaving the island for good. She couldn't say about Jodie. In moments of calmer reflection, she was committed to a shared but unequal custody that would keep Jodie with her for the school year—an absolute must—but would give her time with her father and Howard kin during summer vacations and every other Christmas. But this morning she didn't want to think about such negotiations. She held Jodie tight as the village receded in the distance, turned into a brown smudge on the horizon, then disappeared altogether.

She turned toward the front of the boat, toward Leah waiting at the mainland ferry dock, toward Momma and Father waiting back home, the crib still set up in her old room from Christmas.

Milton Keynes UK
Ingram Content Group UK Ltd.
UKHW021121111124
451035UK00016B/1158